Can You Keep a Secret?

Can You Keep a Secret?

Ten Stories About Secrets

Edited by Lois Metzger

Scholastic Inc.

New York Toronto London Auckland Sydney
Mexico City New Delhi Hong Kong Buenos Aires

ISBN-13: 978-0-439-88022-0
ISBN-10: 0-439-88022-X

12 11 10 9 8 7 6 5 4   7 8 9 10 11 12/0

Printed in the U.S.A.

First Scholastic printing, January 2007

Contents

Can You Keep a Secret?

Foreword

What is a secret?

Knowing something that others don't know.

Keeping something hidden and making sure that others never find out.

Protecting a friend, a family member, someone you barely know.

Why is it sometimes so *hard* to keep a secret?

Because it can be thrilling, even powerful, to have a secret.

And it's a kind of test.

Are you worthy of the secret? Will you be loyal, and keep it always? Will you hurt or disappoint someone if you blurt it out? Or will it be worse if you *don't* tell?

These ten exciting stories, written especially for this book, present ten wholly different ways to think about secrets. For example, Elizabeth Cody Kimmel's story follows a girl who mistakenly asks the wrong boy to a dance—and keeping this information to herself has consequences she never dreamed of. In

Nancy Farmer's story, a girl learns the secret to a curse that has haunted her all her life. In Lulu Delacre's story, a girl learns that keeping a secret is what will help her become the woman she is meant to be. And in Nancy Werlin's story, a girl must give up her secret so she can find her true self.

Some of the stories are realistic; others are fantasy. Some are full of hilarious misunderstandings and misadventures. In others, secrets are serious business.

All of them may start you thinking about your own secrets, secrets entrusted to you, secrets you've entrusted to others, secrets you've found out accidentally, secrets you were always meant to know...and secrets you have yet to discover.

—Lois Metzger

Who Do You Like?

by Nancy Werlin

Steffie sat on the floor of Olivia's beige-and-aqua striped bedroom with her legs outstretched and her back propped up against Olivia's bureau. She glanced around. Marlee was leaning back on her hands on the rug across from Steffie, while Emily had taken the room's only chair. Parvati, meanwhile, had seated herself cross-legged by the foot of the bed.

It went without saying that only Olivia got to sit on the bed, which was draped in aqua to match the walls.

All the other girls were looking expectantly at Olivia. They were waiting for Olivia's Monday after-school question. And it came, same as always, because Olivia was interested in only one thing, and she was the girl in charge of their little group of five.

"So, who do you *like*?" Olivia said. She had her recycled paper notebook open, with her feather pen poised in one hand.

This week, Steffie was ready with an answer. She had the name of a new TV actor she'd read about in *Teen People*. She'd even brought the magazine so they could all see his picture. He was truly gorgeous, so maybe this time she wouldn't be accused of not trying. Of not caring.

Secretly, of course, she didn't. Secretly, Steffie had never liked any of the boys she claimed to like on these Mondays at Olivia's.

Olivia wasn't looking at Steffie yet. "Marlee? It was Jacob Schubert for you last week."

"I still like Jacob," said Marlee. "He's so cute! Put him down again for me."

There was a pause.

"Okay," Olivia said finally. "I will. But you know the rules. You're only allowed to name the same boy three times. By then, something has to have *happened* between you and him, or you have to move on."

Marlee's forehead creased with thought. As Marlee looked around at all of them, she said, "Well, today in the cafeteria, Jacob smiled at me. So that was something that happened. Wasn't it?"

Emily and Parvati and Marlee nodded. Steffie hid a smile.

Olivia leaned forward. "Who smiled *first*?"

"Uh . . ."

Olivia sighed. "Marlee, listen. You need a *plan*. You have to make him *notice* you somehow. Like, last week you said you were going to buy and learn that Xbox game so you'd have something to talk to him about. Did you do it?"

"Uh . . ."

"Marlee!"

"All right, Olivia," said Marlee. "I'll talk to him this week. I promise."

Yeah, Steffie thought. *You'll say hi and so will he. And that'll be that.*

She glanced across the bedroom to where Parvati was. Sometimes, Steffie wondered if Parvati was as frustrated and bored by these weekly meetings as Steffie was. Parvati had it easy, though. She had explained to Olivia that her parents wouldn't allow her to date for many years, if ever. That was the way it was in India, and Parvati's family was very traditional even though they lived in the United States now.

"Then you can just *like* various boys, Parvati," Olivia had decided. "You don't have to *do* anything."

"I will keep it to the movie stars," Parvati had promised, laughing. "That will be safe for me."

Steffie wished she had a consistently safe option, too. But she didn't come from a traditional Indian culture, and she hadn't been able to think of another way out. Not without making Olivia mad, anyway. And losing her friends. Her only girlfriends.

Olivia had moved on now to quizzing Emily. Emily was making actual progress with Patrick Wyzlowski. "We're going to be partners for the science fair," Emily said. She giggled. "I'm invited to his house tomorrow after school for planning!"

"That's great!" said Olivia. "Just the two of you."

"Well…" Emily twisted a strand of red hair around her finger, and then suddenly it was in her mouth. "Actually, there are three of us working on the project together. They were a pair first. But then Patrick asked me to join them."

"Who's the other?" asked Olivia.

"Well …" Emily was chewing her hair like mad. "It's Quentin Karas."

Steffie felt every nerve in her body go on alert.

Olivia rolled her eyes. "Quentin Karas? That skinny, ugly, *dorky* boy? You're kidding me. Right?"

"Patrick will be there. It's his house," Emily said.

Emily! Say Quentin is smart, thought Steffie. *Tell Olivia you want him on the team because he's smart and nice and good to work with. Say that Patrick likes him, hangs out with him sometimes. If Patrick's okay, how come Quentin isn't?*

But Emily didn't say any of those things. And Steffie didn't, either. She just watched as Olivia treated all of them to an imitation of Quentin Karas: the way he jerked his head to one side when he talked, sometimes; the way he could go on and on in class about something if he was interested in it.

Steffie hugged her knees. *Stop, stop, stop,* she thought. *Please stop.*

Olivia and Marlee and Parvati and Emily were some of the nicest girls in the sixth grade, Steffie reminded herself. She was lucky they'd been so welcoming when she'd moved to town only two months ago. She was lucky that Olivia and her group had accepted her.

Beggars can't be choosers, she thought. That was something Steffie's mom said sometimes. Steffie was a social beggar. And Quentin Karas—well, he was a social disaster. Steffie had known it since she first met him, after she and her mom moved in next door. Nobody could look at Quentin and not know it. He wasn't cute. He was too intense and smart. And yes, he was as thin as a stick.

It was nobody's fault. It was just the way things were.

Finally, Olivia stopped her imitation. "Your turn, Steffie," said Olivia.

Steffie took a deep breath. She took out the magazine. "Look at this cool guy," she said, faking eagerness. "He's on that new show, you know? The one on Friday nights?"

There was a little silence. Then, "Oh, Steffie. You picked *another* TV star instead of a real boy at our school?"

What followed was a five-minute lecture from Olivia. Steffie tried, when it was over, to defend herself. "Listen," she said. "I'm still new here. I just can't—I don't know that many boys."

"You can *get* to know some of them," Olivia said sternly. "You just have to try. Take it one by one."

"But I—"

"In fact," said Olivia, "I won't give you a whole *week* this time. That's not doing you any good. You have to get moving, Steffie. So, you have until Wednesday." She waved her feather pen in the air. "I want an acceptable boy's name from you by Wednesday at three o'clock. And I want a *plan* with it."

Steffie stared hopelessly at Olivia. She could feel a headache coming on.

"Okay?" said Olivia.

"Okay," Steffie said faintly.

* * *

Back home that afternoon, Steffie went outside. She pretended to herself that she just wanted to do her reading for English class on the deck. But, really, she was listening. And soon she heard what she had hoped to hear: the pounding of a hammer. She grabbed her book and sprinted down the steps of the deck, heading for the big oak tree on the edge of the yard. There, a well-used pair of New Balance sneakers dangled from a wooden platform five feet above her head. She waited for a pause in the hammering and then yelled up toward the feet.

"Quentin?"

A moment later, the thin, bespectacled face of Quentin Karas appeared over the edge of the platform. He grinned. "Hey, Stef. You coming up?"

"Yeah." With the ease of someone who has done it many times before, Steffie hoisted herself up onto the platform in the tree. She sat with her legs crossed and watched Quentin resume hammering. He was working on a roof for the little tree house, layering on shingles in a neat pattern. Quentin's thin arms arranged and hammered each shingle competently. He was totally occupied by his task. He had told Steffie, back when she'd just moved in next door, that it was his goal to eventually have a perfect, tiny little house up in this tree. He had even picked out paint colors. Steffie had volunteered to help with that part of the project.

"Looking good," Steffie said finally.

Quentin looked over at her and grinned. His smile lit up his whole face. It was one of the things Steffie liked about him, how he didn't hide his feelings. "Thanks," he said. "I found the shingles in the basement the other day."

"Lucky," said Steffie.

"Yeah!"

Quentin went back to work, and Steffie read her book for English. Occasionally, they would look up at each other, but neither of them said another word. It wasn't necessary.

It was peaceful. It was undemanding. And, without doubt, it was the best part of Steffie's Monday.

The next day, Steffie checked out the boys in the sixth and seventh grades, looking for someone she could like.

There had to be *someone*, if she'd just try. Right?

Aaron Knudsen was an obvious choice. He was the tallest boy in the sixth grade. He was cute and popular, and he had the kind of thick blond hair you really did want to touch. Olivia had chosen him herself in the past, twice. The problem, for Steffie, was that Aaron hardly ever stopped talking. There was a constant stream of noise from him—jokes, opinions, laughter. Even when the teacher was talking, Aaron was usually whispering something to someone near him. It was so annoying.

Then there was Nathaniel Ross, a seventh grader. He was so cool; Olivia would approve. But two weeks ago at the mall, while she was shopping for jeans, Steffie had seen Nathaniel spend minutes in front of a three-way mirror, checking himself out. At one point, he struck a kind of pose, as if he were playing air guitar. Steffie had had to press her hand over her mouth so she wouldn't snort out loud.

As she went through the day, she thought about each boy she saw. But there was something wrong with every one of them. Too short. Too scary. Too shy. Too mean. Too immature, or too mature. Smelled weird. Swore too much. Not cute, for one reason or another. There was even one boy who was just too irritatingly nice!

And, of course, there were a few boys who were simply too dorky to be potential *liking* material. They might be nice, or smart, but they weren't worth even thinking about, because Olivia would never accept one of them, never write them down in her recycled paper notebook with her feather pen.

Like Quentin.

At school, Quentin hung out with his small posse

of social misfits. That he and Steffie were friends at home, in privacy, was a secret so deep they never even spoke of it between themselves.

Before today, Steffie had just been grateful that it wasn't an issue. Quentin seemed to understand that their friendship was private, and he didn't even try to be friends at school. But, as she considered all the boys one by one and realized that if she were truly honest, Quentin was the only one she liked—maybe not *liked*, but liked—she suddenly wondered: *Did Quentin mind that she never talked to him at school?*

Did Quentin maybe think Steffie was like Olivia, because she hung out with her?

Wait. *Was* she like Olivia? And even if she wasn't, would she *become* like her, if she continued to hang out with her and accept her rules?

Steffie stuck her head into her mom's office when she got home from school. "Mom?" she said. "May I talk to you for a minute?"

"Sure." Steffie's mom looked up from her computer, where she was doing the quarterly tax return for Romeo's Pizzeria. "I was just thinking I wanted a break. What's up?"

Steffie flung herself into the chair her mom kept for clients. "Oh. I don't know. I guess I wanted to ask your opinion. You know how I'm friends with Quentin, right?"

"Yes, of course."

"Well . . ." Steffie laced her fingers together in her lap and looked down at them. "The thing is, Quentin and I pretend to hardly know each other at school. Like, we never talk or anything. We're only friends here, at home."

"Really?" Steffie's mom leaned forward. "Why's that, sweet pea?"

"I don't know." Steffie paused. "Well, he's sort of a geek. And, well, Olivia . . ." She couldn't quite finish. She watched her interlaced fingers some more. Finally, she looked up at her mom.

Her mom was looking at her gravely. "Olivia's in charge of who is and isn't your friend?"

"No. Well. Yes. I suppose she is." Steffie could feel that her cheeks were red.

"Hm," said her mom.

For a little while, there was silence in the office, and then Steffie burst out, "That's bad, isn't it? I just realized today that it was very bad. It's sort of—well, it's sort of dishonest of me. Isn't it? Because I really like Quentin. I like him better than Olivia, actually. I don't mean *like* like. You know. But I *like* him. He's a good person."

Steffie's mom got up from her chair, walked over to Steffie, and hugged her. "What does Quentin think of this?" she asked.

"I don't actually know."

More silence.

"I guess I need to find out," said Steffie.

"Good girl," said Steffie's mom.

Out in the yard, Steffie couldn't hear any pounding, but she went over to the oak tree, anyway. Today, there were no dangling sneakers, but she called a hello and climbed up onto the platform. Quentin was there, drawing something on graph paper. He waved at her.

"Hey, Stef."

"Hey." She thought she knew what she wanted to say, but she couldn't find the words at first. She sat down, feeling a little awkward. "What are you doing?"

Quentin leaned over and showed Steffie the drawing he was making. "I need to figure out the beam structure to support the tree-house roof. I probably should have thought about this first. I just got all excited when I found those roof shingles in the basement, so I skipped some steps. It was really dumb of me."

"You're not dumb," Steffie said quickly. She felt weirdly indignant.

"I didn't say I was," said Quentin. He gave her a puzzled look. "Just that I did a dumb thing."

"Oh," said Steffie. She could feel herself starting to blush again. And then, suddenly, she knew how to say what she wanted to. She said it fast, before she could get any more nervous. "Listen, Quentin? I've been doing a dumb thing, too."

Quentin had leaned back comfortably against the central trunk of the oak tree and started drawing again. He looked up at her attentively. "What's that?"

"Olivia," Steffie said starkly. "Listening to Olivia."

"Oh," said Quentin.

From the very beginning of their friendship, when Steffie had moved in next door, she and Quentin had never had to say very much in order to understand each other. And as she looked at Quentin now and saw him meet her eyes right back, straight on, direct, she knew that they didn't need to say much now, either.

"I'm wondering," said Steffie. "If we could be friends at school, too. You and me. Or would your friends be mad at you?"

There was a little pause. Then Quentin said, with

the straightforward honesty that Steffie so much liked in him, "My friends would like you, Stef, if they knew you."

"I bet I'd like them, too," said Steffie.

That evening after dinner, Steffie got permission to walk over to Olivia's house. Olivia herself came to the door when Steffie rang the bell. "Steffie? What a surprise! You look a little weird. Is something wrong?"

"No," said Steffie. She was feeling awkward but determined. "Nothing's wrong. It's that—well, I wanted to talk to you about, you know, who I like. Privately."

Olivia was delighted. "Come in! Come up to my room! It's a secret? I should have guessed. You didn't want to say in front of Emily and Parvati and Marlee."

They went up to the aqua-and-beige bedroom. Olivia grabbed her notebook and feather pen and sat down on the edge of her bed, looking expectant and even a little excited. "It's Aaron Knudsen, isn't it? I saw you looking at him today. You're shy about it because you know I used to like him. Right?"

"No," said Steffie. She sat down beside Olivia, something she'd never dared to do before. "That's not it."

"Who, then? Who do you like?"

"It's not who I like," said Steffie. "It's what I like."

"Huh?"

"I don't—I don't . . ." Steffie stuttered.

And then her hands took over for her. She reached over and took the pretty notebook made of recycled paper out of Olivia's hands. She turned to the page that said STEFFIE at the top. And she tore it out.

"Steffie!" Olivia screamed. She grabbed the book back from Steffie.

Steffie stared at the torn page in her hands. Then, slowly, she looked up at Olivia, whose eyes were narrowing.

Steffie's voice came out a little strangled, but clear. "I'm sorry, Olivia," said Steffie. "But listen. This is the truth. I have to tell you. I don't like anybody. Not anybody! Not the way you mean. And I don't want to pretend about it anymore. I—I can't."

The two girls stared at each other.

"Fine," Olivia said tightly, after a while. "That's fine with me."

Steffie stood up. "I'm sorry," she said. "I had to be honest." Uncertainly, she put the STEFFIE page in her pocket. "I'll leave now," said Steffie.

"Good idea," said Olivia.

As Steffie walked away, she could feel Olivia's eyes following her. But Olivia didn't say anything else, and neither did Steffie. And then the door to Olivia's house closed behind Steffie.

And Steffie walked on, alone. She felt awful. And, yet, she also felt . . .

Clean. Like she could take in a deep breath for the first time in a long while.

She walked home slowly. It was a beautiful evening, with stars filling the sky. It was strange to think about school tomorrow. She had to admit she was a little afraid. It would be almost like moving here again, like starting again. Making new friends at school. And dealing with whatever happened as a result of what she had done tonight.

It would be hard. Steffie knew it would be hard.

But this time, no matter what, she wouldn't keep secrets about who she liked.

Or who she was.

The Post-it Malfunction

by Elizabeth Cody Kimmel

Louisa had gotten into the mess herself, with a little help from Sadie Hawkins, and she was simply going to have to keep it a secret for the whole night. Even it if killed her.

It had happened just two days before the dance, in morning meeting during homeroom. Louisa was gazing dreamily at Luke when the announcement was made. Luke of the honey-colored hair and Hershey brown eyes. Luke of the varsity jacket and faded crimson high-tops. Luscious Luke, the object of every sane seventh-grade girl's hopes and dreams.

"Which is why," Mrs. McFeely was droning in her sinus-plagued voice, "we have decided to have the seventh grade's very first Sadie Hawkins Dance!"

Louisa heard these words vaguely. She didn't

recognize the name *Sadie Hawkins*. Maybe she was a new girl, transferring into the class at that awkward mid-year point. Louisa glanced across the room at her best friend, Tess, and together they rolled their eyes. Louisa didn't care about a new girl. She didn't care about anything at the moment but the back of Luscious Luke's head. Unless, Louisa thought suddenly, gripping the desk, this new girl, this Sadie Hawkins, turned out to be some kind of world-class babe! Oh, no! What if Luke met Sadie, and it was love at first sight?

"For those of you who don't know," Mrs. McFeely continued, "Sadie Hawkins was actually the name of a character in a comic strip."

A character in a comic strip? This seemed to lessen the chances that Sadie was destined to become the object of Luke's affection. Louisa began to listen to Mrs. McFeely more closely.

"A Sadie Hawkins dance," Mrs. McFeely continued, "is one in which it is traditional, and in fact *required*, that the *boy* be invited by the *girl*. It's a fairness issue, really. A chance for the girls to invite someone to a dance without feeling they need to *wait* to be asked. In all other ways, this dance will be just like our Fall Frolic and our Christmas Cotillion. Only the invitation process will be different. Please let me know if any of you have parents available to chaperone."

Across the classroom, Tess was miming a person gasping for air and simultaneously making discreet gestures in Luke's direction. Tess had been trying for three months to assist in getting the crush-stricken Louisa within ten feet of Luke, without success. Louisa made the "shut up!!!" signal to Tess, and plopped her head down on her desk. The world was spinning, and Louisa had a sneaking suspicion that her face had turned either very white, or very red. Maybe an unflattering combination of both.

This is a nightmare, Louisa thought, still hiding her face.

If she didn't ask Luke, and do it practically instantaneously, another girl (or twenty) was sure to. He was, after all, *perfection*. Louisa had the advantage, because Luke was right here in her homeroom, just a few desks away. Louisa knew of three other girls, Doreen Tschinklett, Meghan Rider, and Valerie Broadenbeam, who also worshipped Luke on a pretty much full-time basis. But none of them was in Mrs. McFeely's homeroom. Louisa could be the first to ask him. But if she did ask Luke, she would be forced by the evil and obviously deranged Sadie Hawkins into having *actual human contact* with him. Possibly even a conversation. For, like, an entire minute. Louisa did not feel confident that she could string together enough words in the correct order to communicate her invitation to Luke without . . . puking.

So that left her the option of writing a note. But she wasn't entirely certain that was a good idea, either. Notes were so . . . forever. You could say something out loud, then say "forget it," or, "just kidding, HAH!" if things were clearly heading for disaster. But a note couldn't be unwritten. It couldn't be taken back once it was delivered. Worst of all, a note could be shown to other people. Theoretically, Luke could show her note to other people. Theoretically, she could become a laughingstock. Theoretically, her seventh-grade life might be doomed.

And while Louisa firmly believed that no one as gorgeous as Luke would be capable of such a diabolical act, it did bear thinking about. So instead of actually writing Luke a real note, she wrote a practice one. A first draft, it would be called in Miss Hinky's creative writing class. She wrote the draft on the only piece of paper she had handy that was small enough to be hidden away—a three-inch-by-three-inch neon green Post-it note. The draft went something like this:

Hey. So anyway, since we have to ask someone to this Hawkins thing, I thought I'd ask you. Since I actually really like you, or whatever, and it would obviously be better to go with a cool guy that I'm into and not some random doof-wad loser. So do you want to go to the dance with me?

Louisa

As soon as she read it, actually *saw* it there in real life in her tiny but precise handwriting, Louisa realized the only doof-wad loser in this scenario was her. The note was pathetic. She peeled the Post-it off the pad and slid it under her pencil case. As soon as the bell rang, she would toss it in the garbage. *No,* she thought, *that would be* stupid! Someone could fish it out of the garbage and read it! Luke's name wasn't on it, but hers was. She would have to get rid of it another way. She would dash into the girls' room and flush the note down the toilet.

Louisa leaped to her feet at first bell, grabbed her stuff, and headed for the restroom so she could flush the note without delay. She was so focused on this task she didn't notice Wally Loppenschmeer, the square-headed advanced-placement Latin merit scholar with the funny-shaped lips, also leaping to his feet at first bell. Louisa should have anticipated this. Everybody knew that Wally Loppenschmeer, with his odd little duck walk and his obsessive devotion to scholastic perfection, had *stomach problems.* He was always darting into the boys' room like his life depended on it. But in Louisa's zeal to dispose of the

Post-it, she had forgotten about Wally Loppen-schmeer altogether. That is, until they collided so forcefully, she literally saw stars and bluebirds circling above her head, just like in cartoons. The shock of the impact left her momentarily insensible.

"Oh, geez! Oh, man! I am so sorry, Louisa! Are you okay? Are you hurt?"

Louisa heard Wally Loppenschmeer's voice as if it were coming from a great distance, or being broadcast through Jell-O. She was still seeing stars and the odd bluebird here and there. As Wally anxiously repeated the question, Louisa looked wildly around the room. Where was Luke? Had he already gotten out the door? In her hurry to get rid of the note, she had forgotten she was back to Plan A. Asking Luke in person. Half the class had already left the room. There was no time to make polite conversation with Wally Loppenschmeer.

"Excuse me," Louisa mumbled, not even making eye contact with Wally. Keeping her gaze toward the floor, she slung her schoolbag over her shoulder and walked quickly (but she dared hope with grace) outside into the hallway. She was just in time to see Luscious Luke disappear around the corner at the end of the hall.

It was too late. She'd blown it. Not even a cheerleader with perfect hair, skin, and nails would run down the hall after a guy to ask him to a dance. She had lost the best opportunity life had ever given her to go to a dance with Luscious Luke.

Louisa leaned on a locker to take a moment and took a deep, cleansing breath. She just needed to collect herself for a minute before getting rid of the note. At that moment, she saw Wally Loppenschmeer dashing out of the classroom. He took off down the hallway at a brisk trot, in the direction of the boys' room.

The neon green Post-it was stuck to his elbow.

The first annual Sadie Hawkins Dance was officially under way. The gym had been transformed by the Decoration Committee into something resembling ... a gym with streamers. Louisa was standing awkwardly by the beverage table with a nervous Wally Loppenschmeer at her side. She tried not to think about how it had come to this. How Wally had found the Post-it on his elbow, read the note, and presumed it was meant for him. How he'd found Louisa by the bus after school, and stammered and mumbled and blushed his way through accepting her invitation to the Sadie Hawkins Dance. How in her embarrassment for them both, and her lack of a backup plan, she'd just gone along with it and nodded. How she was now here at a dance as Wally's date because of a Post-it malfunction.

"Um, some cherry-berry spritzer? Louisa?" Wally asked. He was trying to be nice. He had obviously made an effort to dress snappily in basic black and denim. Louisa sighed unhappily.

Why had he thought she had really meant to ask him to the dance? What kind of idiot delivered an invitation to someone's *elbow*? You had to be really smart to get into advanced-placement Latin. Couldn't Wally have figured out that it was a mistake? Yes, Louisa knew that the mix-up was almost all her fault. Yes, she had neglected to put Luke's name on the note. It was Louisa's mess, and she firmly intended to treat Wally with the utmost politeness, because that's how she'd want to be treated if their positions were switched. But it was just so frustrating.

"Oh, yeah, you know, whatever," Louisa said. "I mean, I'm okay."

"You're okay with some cherry-berry spritzer?" Wally pressed. "Or you're okay without it? There's another pitcher, too, with something else in it. It looks like Gatorade. The cherry-berry spritzer looks better."

Something about hearing Wally say "cherry-berry

spritzer" struck Louisa as funny. She usually only heard him talk in class, when he sounded like a textbook, or once in a special assembly, when he conjugated Latin verbs while simultaneously translating them into sign language. She had a sudden, probably insane wish to hear him say it one more time.

"I guess I . . . well, keeping hydrated is very important I know, but . . . which one did you say looks better?"

"The cherry-berry spritzer," Wally replied patiently.

Really, he's not a bad sport, Louisa thought, discreetly scanning the room for Luke. She still didn't know who had asked Luke to the dance. Tess didn't know. Nobody seemed to know. "You know, Wally, I think I will have a cherry-berry spritzer," Louisa said. Then she looked over at him and smiled.

Louisa wasn't faking being pleasant to Wally. And it wasn't entirely because of the Post-it malfunction. Wally had a kind of earnestness that made Louisa, to her surprise, really *want* to be nice to him. But the Post-it was a big part of it, too. Louisa was painfully aware that Wally thought she "really liked" him, because that's what the stupid note had said.

Poor guy, Louisa thought. He'd be so embarrassed if he knew the truth. He'd probably never come back to school again, just from the shame. Louisa wouldn't wish that kind of humiliation on anyone, including Wally Loppenschmeer. The Post-it malfunction had to remain a secret. And when they were back in school on Monday? If Wally, like, wanted to hang out? Or if he asked her to go for ice cream or something? She'd say something gentle, but firm. She had rehearsed many options already. Her current favorite was, "I just need to focus on myself right now. It isn't you, Wally, it's me." Not mean, but a definite *no*.

"Here you go," Wally said, handing Louisa a plastic cup full of red liquid.

"Thank you, Wally," Louisa said. And she tried to give him a look that included kindness and goodwill toward Wally and the entire human race in general, but that did not include liking in a girl-likes-boy kind of way. To stress her gratitude for the punch, Louisa downed it in one sip.

"Wow," Wally exclaimed. "Impressive. Should we dance now?"

Oh, good grief. She hadn't meant to pave the way for a trip to the dance floor. But now Wally had asked, and she didn't want him to feel bad. There'd be time enough for that when she had to let him down easy at school on Monday.

"Sure," Louisa said. They walked together to the center of the gym, where a little cluster of rainbow-colored streamers dangled high above them. Not too many people were dancing yet. Louisa pretended to scratch a place between her shoulder blades, while actually looking around for Luke. She didn't see him, but she did catch sight of Tess and her date, who also happened to be Tess's cousin. Tess caught Louisa's eye and began to mime a person staggering around being sick to her stomach. Louisa looked away quickly and was relieved to see Wally busy with straightening his glasses, and not noticing Tess at all.

There was a good song playing, something by the Arctic Monkeys. Wally started to dance and, at first, Louisa thought he looked like he was trying to shake a centipede off each sleeve. She did a little bounce-step thing to the right, and to the left, keeping her eyes off of Wally, and checking for Luke in every corner. Where was he, anyway? Louisa had resigned herself to her evening with Wally, but she wanted, she simply *had* to know what lucky girl had gotten to Luke in time. When she looked back at Wally, she was surprised to find he really didn't look so bad dancing. Actually, he was kind of *good*.

"I love the Arctic Monkeys," Wally said, just before executing a little spin that brought him around in a circle perfectly.

"You *do*?" Louisa asked. She hadn't meant to sound so surprised, but she thought advanced-placement Latin merit scholars listened more to orchestra stuff and things with opera singers. Smart-people music. Dead-people music.

Wally didn't answer, but instead he lifted up on his tippy toes and did a rapid back-and-forth shuffle that should have looked ridiculous, but came off as downright impressive.

"Wow!" Louisa exclaimed. "Where did you learn that?"

Wally shrugged, then grinned and skipped his feet out and in to the song's now somewhat frenzied beat. The more Louisa noticed Wally's dance moves, the more self-conscious she became about her own dancing, which seemed pretty lame in comparison. Anyway, what if Luke saw? She didn't want to look like she was having fun. When the song ended, Wally didn't look a bit tired.

"Some of that cherry-berry spritzer might go down pretty well around now," Louisa said quickly, before the next song started. She said it mostly to get them off the dance floor, but she also wanted Wally to feel good about his beverage-providing services. Anyway, they'd get a better view of the gym from there. Surely, she'd be able to spot Luke soon.

They didn't really say anything on the way back to the snack table. Louisa glanced up at the big clock on the wall, the one with a metal cage over it to protect it from wayward basketballs. She was surprised to find they had been at the dance for almost an hour. Louisa had expected the evening to drag unbearably, but now there were only about ninety minutes left to go before her parents would be picking her up. This really wasn't so bad.

Wally handed Louisa a cup and a brownie, and she pretended to take a long sip of punch as she examined the gym from one end to the other. How was it possible she could not see Luke?

"He's actually not coming, I think," Wally said.

Louisa started to nod automatically, then snapped into reality and did a classic double take. Wally gazed back at her, his eyes clear.

"What? Who's not coming?"

Wally looked down at his feet.

"I'm sorry," he said. "I just sort of assumed you were looking for Luke."

"Luke?" Louisa said, trying to sound as if she wasn't sure she could place a face to that name. Her voice had the most stupidly fake ring she had ever heard in her life. "Luke from . . . homeroom?"

Yikes, Louisa thought. *Please rewind and ERASE.*

"It's just that I heard he's not coming, if that was . . . of any interest to you."

"Yeah, no, I mean it isn't, or anything, you know," Louisa said rapidly. She could not have sounded less convincing if she tried. *Drop it*, she told herself. *Change the subject immediately.* "So . . . why isn't he here? Just out of, like, curiosity." *Please tell me that was not MY VOICE asking that question,* Louisa thought. But it was. She couldn't help herself. She had to know why Luke wasn't coming. She bit into the brownie ferociously, to make it more difficult for her to say any more stupid things.

"I heard something like, seven or eight girls asked Luke to the dance. And he told every single one he was already going with somebody else. But he wasn't going with anyone else, because the one girl he wanted to go to the dance with never invited him."

Louisa swallowed her bite of brownie. She wanted to grab Wally by both shoulders (gosh, she hadn't realized how *tall* he was) and demand that he produce the names of those eight girls. Maybe then she could identify that "one girl." Instead, trying to act all casual, she said, "Bizarre. How do you know?"

Wally grinned and took off his glasses, polishing the lenses with his shirt before replacing them. His eyes, Louisa realized suddenly, were *green.*

"You'd be surprised what we hear in AP Latin," Wally said, waggling his eyebrows up and down for emphasis. "Two of the girls he turned down are in the class. And they had classes with some of the other girls, so they figured it out when they compared notes. They were kind of irritated that he lied. People aren't stupid."

Louisa nodded. No, people weren't stupid. She was desperately trying to remember if Valerie Broadenbeam was in AP Latin or AP French. If Valerie was one of the eight, that only left seven . . .

"Louisa?" Wally asked. He touched her on the arm to get her attention, but she was temporarily zoned out, trying to figure out who Luke had rejected, and who he might have been waiting for.

"Louisa?" Wally repeated. He stepped a little closer.

"Sorry, what?" Louisa asked. *Snap out of it*, she told herself.

"No, it's just that you have something stuck to you, there." Wally said. "There," he repeated, pointing.

He was pointing to a place about halfway down her arm. She twisted her elbow around and saw what was stuck to her.

It was a neon green Post-it note.

"I thought you might want that back," Wally said, blushing slightly. He took a long sip of cherry-berry spritzer and peered at her over the rim of the cup.

Her mouth hanging open in shock, Louisa peeled off the note and saw her own small, familiar handwriting. She stared at Wally, genuinely speechless.

He put his cup down on the snack table, shrugged, and smiled.

"Look, it's okay," Wally said. "I know you didn't mean for the note to go to me. Tess kind of . . . explained."

That fink! What was Tess's problem? She had promised to let Louisa handle the Post-it malfunction her own way. Being appointed the official Louisa-Luke matchmaker had apparently gone to Tess's head.

"I am so sorry. That was supposed to be a secret!" Louisa began, but Wally stopped her.

"No, listen, you have absolutely NOTHING to be sorry for. I knew that note wasn't for me before Tess spelled it out. I mean, come on. A girl like you asking someone like . . . well. Anyway. But she did kind of let slip who the note really was for. And then I heard about Luke turning down girls right and left. I guess it made me kind of mad. And I got this crazy idea that I should give it a shot—pretend you had asked me. I shouldn't have done that, Louisa. It just seemed like it might be my only chance to ever go to a dance with you. I had no idea how cool you'd end up being about it."

Louisa's mind was going a mile a minute. Who knew Luscious Luke could be so . . . shallow? He could have turned her down, too. Number nine. She would have been *mortified*.

"So I figure we have two options here. We can just stop hanging out now, no hard feelings. Or . . . we could dance again."

Unless . . . could it have been *Louisa* that Luke had been waiting for? Did she dare to think she could be the reason he wasn't here?

"Louisa?" Wally asked. Louisa suddenly remembered that Wally was in the universe. That not only was he in the universe, that he was standing two feet away from her. That he had just asked her to dance. Not a Post-it malfunction dance, but a *real* dance.

"Sorry, yeah, no," she said. "Yeah, no, Wally, that's . . ."

He stood patiently, waiting for her to get past saying yeah and no in the same sentence. She had her gentle letdown prepared. She didn't have to blow it a second time, blurting out yes when she meant no. She took a deep breath.

Wally's head really wasn't square at all, Louisa noticed as she prepared to answer. It was actually kind of noble looking. And those lips she always thought were funny-shaped looked nice in the half smile Wally wore. Whatever might have happened, it really hadn't ended up being such a bad thing that a Post-it malfunction had set her up with Wally Loppenschmeer. Not so bad at all.

"It's okay," Wally said. "Let's just . . . you know. Just give me a yes or no. To make sure it's clear."

Louisa opened her mouth to form the *N* that in most languages begins the sound meaning *no.*

"Yes," she said. And then, just to make Wally laugh, she stuck the Post-it smack in the middle of his forehead.

A Lump of Clay

by Anne Mazer

"Remember, Class: Beauty, Harmony, and Proportion," Mr. Weevil, the art teacher, droned. "That is what makes Art."

He continued, "I want you to put Beauty, Harmony, and Proportion in your sculptures today. Just like the ancient Greeks did."

Elise turned to her best friend, Sara. "How am I supposed to do that?" she groaned. She frowned at the block of clay on her desk.

There were similar blocks of clay on every desk in the classroom. They were gray, chunky, and plain. They reminded Elise of big blocky apartment buildings without any windows.

"Elise! *You* need Preparation BHP," Sara said, trying to sound like a television announcer. "Just rub a teaspoon of this miracle cream into your artwork and amaze even the ancient Greeks! Beauty, Harmony, and Proportion guaranteed or your money back."

She was going to say more, but Mr. Weevil shot her a look.

There was no fooling around in Mr. Weevil's class. He especially didn't like it when students like Sara tried to liven things up with some harmless humor.

Mr. Weevil pointed to the examples of Greek art and sculpture on the wall. "Study these," he said to the class. "They will help you create a masterpiece."

"Who is he kidding?" Elise said. "There's no way I'm going to create a masterpiece."

"You'll be lucky to complete the assignment," Sara said.

Elise shrugged. It was true. She wasn't very good at art, and even worse at Art.

But she checked out the pictures, anyway. They were mildly interesting. She especially liked the tall white marble columns, the heads with their noses broken off, and the boy trying to get something out of his foot.

"Has he tried tweezers?" Sara said.

Elise suppressed a giggle.

"Class, are you ready?" Mr. Weevil's fingers

twitched, as if they couldn't wait to start creating Beauty.

Sara grabbed her block of clay and dramatically kissed it. "I'm ready, Mr. Weevil."

"Sara, this is your last chance. One more outbreak and you're going to the principal's office."

"But, Mr. Weevil, I'm just getting in the creative mood," Sara protested.

This time, everyone in the class laughed. Elise was proud that Sara was her best friend. No one else in the class was so courageous or so funny.

Mr. Weevil's face turned bright pink. But he didn't send Sara to the principal's office.

Sara always got away with things.

Elise wished she had Sara's nerve—not to mention her humor. Maybe some of it would rub off on her someday.

The class quieted down as the students began to knead their blocks of clay.

"Remember the ancient Greeks," Mr. Weevil intoned.

"Will I ever," Sara muttered. She started to sculpt a woman, deliberately breaking off the nose and arms.

"What's Mr. Weevil going to say?" Elise asked anxiously.

"Nothing," Sara said. "It's just like the ancient Greek statues."

"Is it?" Elise asked. *It was one thing when Time broke off the arms or legs of a perfect statue,* she thought. *It was another when a person broke off pieces to make her sculpture look old.*

But at least Sara was doing something. At least she had ideas.

Elise's own block of clay sat there untouched, as if challenging Elise to make it into anything more than a sullen lump.

Elise tore off a piece of clay and began to knead it. It felt surprisingly good under her fingers. She forgot about her worries and concentrated on the clay—pounding and rolling until the entire block was round, supple, and smooth.

Her hands felt warm and strong and full of energy. That was a new feeling. Elise glanced around the room.

The other kids in the class were sculpting vases, heads, and columns.

There wasn't much Beauty, little Harmony, and only occasional Proportion. Did Mr. Weevil really expect them from a sixth-grade class?

Elise kneaded her clay. She felt as if sunshine was flooding through her hands. She felt as if she was giving life to the clay. Or was it the other way around?

Time stopped. The room vanished. Was this how the ancient Greeks felt when they were making *their* sculptures?

But then Sara broke the spell. She had finished her figure in record time. No wonder. It didn't have arms, legs, or a nose.

She turned to Elise. "Show me what you made."

Elise's hands involuntarily covered the clay. She wanted to protect the new life forming under her hands. Even from Sara.

"What's the big secret?"

"Nothing. No secret."

"Animal, vegetable, or human?" Sara asked.

Elise didn't usually keep secrets from Sara. Elise glanced down at her hands and didn't say anything.

"You made *nothing*? Just a lump of clay?"

Elise made an irritated noise. Sara didn't understand. She needed to leave Elise alone with the clay. Why was her best friend so insensitive?

Stop it, she told herself. Sara was just being herself. And Elise was acting like Mr. Weevil. No sense of humor.

All the while, her hands kept on shaping the clay. Her hands were definitely in charge. They had a life independent of hers. All she had to do was to let them do what they wanted.

Then, abruptly, they stopped moving. Elise drew in a long breath. She was almost afraid to see what she had created.

Slowly, she pulled her hands away and looked down.

A funny little man with a wide nose and curious eyes stared up at her. He was wearing a garland of leaves around his head and a kind of flowing garment that reached to his knees. His shoulders were huge and muscular. And he distinctly looked as if he were laughing at her.

Elise didn't know if the clay figurine had Beauty, Proportion, and Harmony. It probably didn't, she guessed.

In what corner of her mind had she ever dreamed she could create that?

Her figurine didn't look anything like an ancient Greek sculpture. But it had *something*. It was . . . well, kind of alive.

Then she noticed Sara. She was staring at the figure in Elise's hand. Her face registered a mixture of horror and fascination.

"What's *that*?" she said.

Elise's fingers closed hard around the little man. And crumpled him in her hand. A sharp, throbbing pain shot through her fingers.

"Like you said. A lump of clay."

"Oh," said Sara.

Elise felt sick inside, as if she had killed someone. Why had she crushed the funny little man? Why was she so afraid of showing him to Sara? What was she ashamed of?

Furious, she began to knead the clay again.

Again, that strange warmth and energy in her hands. They pounded and smoothed and shaped until the clay was humming.

"You'd better do something," Sara warned. "Mr. Weevil will give you a failing grade if you don't."

Elise barely heard her.

This time, her hands moved faster. It was done in only minutes. And there he stood again. The funny little man with his huge shoulders, garland of leaves, and curious eyes. She hadn't destroyed him at all.

He seemed a bit annoyed. As if he hadn't enjoyed being turned back into a lump of clay.

"Sorry," Elise whispered.

Was it her imagination or did he scowl?

A shadow fell across her desk. It was Mr. Weevil, checking on the students' progress.

"Beauty, Proportion, and Harmony," he droned. "Remember that, budding artists."

Budding artist? Did he think she was a tree?

Elise smiled to herself. She'd have to tell that one to Sara. But she made sure to cup her hands so that

Mr. Weevil wouldn't see the humorous little man.

Or, rather, the annoyed little man. He was definitely scowling at her now.

"What are you hiding, Elise?" Mr. Weevil said. "A masterpiece?" His mouth twitched in amusement.

Sara laughed loudly at his joke. Too loudly.

What was wrong with her today, anyway?

"Well?" Mr. Weevil demanded.

"Um," Elise said. She clutched the tiny figure in her hand. Too tightly. Pain shot through her hands and arms. She had done it again!

Why did she keep destroying him? She didn't mean to. Really!

"I don't have anything to show, Mr. Weevil," she said, heartsick at what she had just done.

"You're in big trouble," Sara said.

Mr. Weevil frowned. "You have eleven minutes to avoid a failing grade," he said, and passed on to the next student.

"Told you," Sara said. Mr. Weevil had given her a C-minus. She was in a bad mood.

"Shut up," Elise muttered. Her hands began to knead the clay.

Oh, please, she prayed. *Come back just one more time. I'll never crumple you up again, I promise.*

The miraculous warmth and light poured through her hands. And for the third time, the little man appeared. The corners of his mouth turned down, his eyes glared, and even his wreath looked upset.

"I won't do it again," she promised. "Really."

The little man seemed to relax. His eyes suddenly lit up with amusement.

"Talking to yourself won't help," Sara said.

Elise ignored her and raised her hand.

"What is it now, Elise?" Mr. Weevil asked.

"I finished the assignment," Elise said.

"Already?" Sara said.

Elise got up and walked to the front of the class, holding the little man cupped in her hands.

"Sit down," Mr. Weevil ordered.

Elise shook her head. For a moment, she just stood there. And then she opened her hands.

A murmur ran through the class.

Sara gasped. For once, she had nothing to say.

"How . . . how did . . . ?" Mr. Weevil stammered. Suddenly stern, he asked, "Did you sneak him into class? Did you steal him?"

"I made him," Elise said, "from a lump of clay."

As she spoke the words, the little man grew larger. He leaped from her hands onto the teacher's desk.

The little man adjusted his wreath and picked up a pointer. He rapped three times on the desk. It split open.

A chasm appeared in the desk. Elise looked down

and saw sheer cliffs and tumbling water. From far below came the sounds of an ancient flute.

The little man smiled. Then, without warning, he leaped into the chasm. The desk slammed shut over him.

Elise trembled from head to foot.

Her classmates were silent as if they had been turned to stone.

Mr. Weevil was the first to speak. "Ah . . . A-plus, young lady, A-plus," he said, and then staggered out of the classroom.

The bell rang, signaling the end of the period.

A-plus, Elise said to herself as she returned to pick up her backpack. *A-plus* . . . she repeated, as if trying it on for size.

A short time ago, she would have been thrilled. A short time ago, she wouldn't have believed her luck. Elise wasn't the kind of person who ever got an A-plus in anything.

Now the A-plus seemed trivial and unimportant.

Back at the desk, Sara avoided her eyes. "How did you do it?" she mumbled, but there was no way for Elise to answer.

Pictures kept flashing in front of her eyes. She saw the little man rap the desk with the pointer. She saw the high rocky cliffs and the water below. And then, she saw him disappear over and over again.

All this had come out of her hands. Or it had come through her hands. Whatever. The truth was, she didn't know how or why it had happened.

The art room was empty now. It was time to move on, but Elise stayed. She stood there, waiting.

Nothing stirred. Worn-out erasers sat in the chalkboard tray. A forgotten book lay on the floor.

Suddenly, she saw it. It was sitting on the next desk—cold, gray, and square. A block of clay. She picked it up and held it in her hands.

It was funny, Elise thought, how a lump of clay could become the dividing point between one life and another. She had crossed an invisible line, and now everything had changed. Her hands began to smooth the sharp edges of the clay, which softened and yielded to her touch. Light and warmth flooded through her.

She wrapped the clay in plastic and placed it in her backpack. With her head held high, Elise strode out of the art room and headed for the next class. *This is just the beginning*, she said to herself.

If You Promise, Never Again

by Lulu Delacre

Tere didn't want to do it. Funny, she had been so eager for this day at the mall with Conchita. And now...

Yesterday before dinner, Conchita had called.

"*¡Hola, nena!* Hi," Conchita Garcia said in that unmistakable tone that, when you heard it, you knew she was showing every single tooth in her mouth. Big smile. "Do you want to go to Plaza tomorrow? Amparito can drop us off."

Tere couldn't believe it. Her mother might just let her. She trusted the Garcias. *Son gente seria*, her mom would say. Serious people, responsible people. Tere knew how important that was to her mom.

Going to the mall with Conchita. Wow! Conchita was really popular in the seventh grade. All the girls flocked to her. And she was the youngest of five siblings, so doing stuff with her meant you didn't have to get driven by your parents. Conchita's sister Amparito was nine years older than Conchita. Amparito could drive them to the mall, which was more fun than being driven by their parents.

"I'd love to," said Tere. "Let me ask my mom, and I'll call you right back."

Plaza las Américas was the largest mall in San Juan—no, actually, on the whole island of Puerto Rico. On Saturdays, lots of girls went there just to walk around, look at the stores, try on some clothes, or go to the movies. It was so nice and cool inside, and you never knew whom you would bump into. It was kind of fun to see and be seen.

Tere hung up the phone and ran downstairs, stumbling into the kitchen. The smell of the kidney-bean stew simmering on the stove made her mouth water.

"Mami, can I go to Plaza with Conchita tomorrow?" Tere asked.

"I don't think so," Tere's mom said. "Tomorrow we're going to visit your grandmother."

"*Por favor*, Mami, please," Tere said, her brown eyes

peeking through her long bangs. "Amparito is driving us."

Her mom sighed and said, "*Está bien*, fine. I guess we can visit your grandmother on Sunday. But you have to be back by six o'clock. And no later."

"*¡Chévere!*" exclaimed Tere, running back upstairs to phone her friend.

After calling Conchita, Tere spent the next hour and a half planning what she would wear. She tried on the red shirt with the bandannalike print, the aqua shirt with the blue glittery stripes, and the pink-and-ivory shirt with tiny bows on its sleeves. She settled on the aqua shirt with her new jeans. That night, Tere had trouble going to sleep. Ahh—a day at the mall! It could be full of surprises.

The next day, the birds feeding in the backyard trees woke up Tere. The noisy birds and the bright sun forcing its way between the wooden slats of the windows were impossible to ignore. Another hot and sunny Saturday in May. It would be good to spend it at the mall.

Downstairs, Tere found her breakfast sitting on the kitchen countertop. She ate the guava pastry eagerly, first licking the thick layer of powdered sugar that covered the top. She washed the pastry down with the hot milk laced with coffee that her mother had fixed for her, and then hurried back to her room to get ready.

Soon the bell rang. Tere smoothed out her pink lip gloss and looked at herself in the mirror one last time.

"Tere!" she heard her mother call. "Conchita is here."

Tere checked her purse before hanging it over her shoulder. Money, keys, lip gloss. All there.

"*¡Hola, Doña Marta!*" Tere heard Conchita say from the landing of the stairs. Conchita had her wavy hair up on one side, fastened with two glittering butterfly clips. The shiny butterflies had lacy wings that fluttered with the slightest movement of Conchita's head. They were really, really pretty.

"*¡Hola, Conchita!*" said Tere's mom with a big smile. You could tell how much her mother liked her friend. *Gente seria.* Tere waved good-bye to her mother and climbed into Amparito's car. In the backseat, she breathed in deeply and smiled a little smile.

Once in Plaza, Tere and Conchita agreed on a time and place to meet Amparito at the end of the day. The mall was packed. Even early in the day, there were tons of kids walking around. Every now and then, Conchita would stop and say hi to someone. She seemed to know lots of people.

Tere looked at her friend and wished she were more like her. Conchita was the outgoing one, the crazy one, the one who could laugh off anything. Tere didn't dare take risks. She was kind of quiet and used to following the rules. They had been best friends in school, from kindergarten until fifth grade. Then, Tere spent sixth grade in a different school. When she returned to the school she had gone to with Conchita, Tere found that her best friend was not her best friend anymore. She was now best friends with many other girls. That was why Tere had been so pleasantly surprised at Conchita's invitation.

"Vente," said Conchita. "Come with me—let's go in here. They have a great makeup section." Conchita went right to the eye-shadow display. There were lots of samples to try on. Conchita applied frosted blue eye shadow on one lid and lavender on the other one. She looked at Tere and laughed that laugh of hers—jingle bells cascading in a crystal vase.

"You're next," Conchita declared.

"No," said Tere. "Mami wouldn't like it."

At that moment, an older woman approached the counter. She wore a pink shirt, and a strong rose perfume seemed to envelope her. Conchita moved over to the section with hair accessories. Tere followed. That is when she saw them.

There—on top of the revolving display, along with barrettes, headbands, and scrunchies, were the butterfly hair clips. The exact same ones Conchita had on. Tere touched them gently. The wings looked so delicate. Tere flipped them over to look at the price on the back: $5.00. *Five dollars?*

"*¿Te gustan?*" asked Conchita. "You like them?"

"*Sí,*" Tere's voice trailed off.

"*¡Llévatelos!* Take them!" Conchita said.

"They're too expensive," said Tere.

Conchita looked around and whispered, "Who says you have to buy them?"

Tere looked at her friend, puzzled. Was Conchita suggesting what Tere thought she was suggesting? Conchita told Tere she had done it herself. It was no big deal. You just put it in your purse real quick.

No, Tere didn't want to do it.

But then—

Maybe that was what it took to be carefree and popular.

First, Tere looked around, and then at her purse. She smelled a faint scent of roses. For a moment, her chest closed up. Tere had to leave the store. Conchita ran after her.

"What's wrong with you?" Conchita said. "Don't you like those clips? We would look alike." Conchita grabbed Tere by the arm. "Open your purse and keep calm. We're going back in there."

Tere found herself opening the zipper of her purse automatically while she listened to Conchita whisper how pretty Tere was going to look with the clips in her hair. Tere stood, again, in front of the display. She truly liked the butterflies. She had ten dollars—her allowance of two months. She could spend half of it on the hair clips, but then she wouldn't be able to go to the movies. Tere felt dizzy.

Conchita squeezed her arm. "Now," she said, "no one is looking."

Tere saw her hand take the clips and slip them into her open purse. She felt there and not there, both at once. Conchita picked up a pack of chewing gum and went to the cashier. Tere followed blindly.

Once they were out of the store and halfway down the wide hallway, Conchita started laughing so hard she had to bend over. "You see how easy that was?" she said.

Tere bit her lower lip and smiled. But suddenly, the scent of roses assaulted her.

"*¡Un momentito, por favor!*" the woman in the pink

shirt called from behind. "One moment, please!" The woman grabbed Tere and Conchita by the arms. "You two have to come with me."

Conchita looked at Tere and shrugged. Tere began to shake, feeling like everyone's eyes were on her. Could this really be happening? The woman took them straight to the store's manager.

"I think you need to have a little chat with these girls, Mr. Ramos. Ask them what this one has in her purse."

Tere felt like melting into the floor and becoming one with the shiny, speckled tiles. Trembling, she took the hair clips out of her purse and handed them to Mr. Ramos.

"What's your name?" Mr. Ramos asked.

"Tere Mendez," she whispered. She could not take her gaze off the floor.

"Mendez?" he asked. "Are you one of Professor Mendez's daughters?"

Did he know her dad? No, it couldn't be possible. Tere nodded yes.

"I was his student in Philosophy 101. I know him well."

Tere felt her face turn crimson and her ears glow with throbbing shame.

"Sit down," Mr. Ramos said as he kicked back

his chair and smoothed his thick black mustache. "Is this the first time you've stolen anything?"

Tere's throat was so dry, it was as if all its moisture had gone to her hands and feet. She looked at Conchita out of the corners of her eyes. *"Sí, señor,"* she said. "Yes, sir. But I didn't want to."

Tere told Mr. Ramos all about how it had happened. When she was done, she breathed in deeply and looked up, a tear running down her cheek.

Mr. Ramos scolded Conchita for pressuring her friend, and then asked her to wait outside. He leaned over his desk, clasped his hands, and looked directly at Tere. "I know you didn't mean to do it," he said. "I don't have to tell your father, you know. We can keep this between us, *nuestro secreto*. If you promise, never again."

Tere wanted to be Conchita's friend. She wanted to be like her. But not at this price. Following her friend's lead had felt wrong all along—she had felt it in her heart. She couldn't imagine what her parents' disappointment would be like when they found out. But—she suddenly realized—they would never find out. As long as she kept her promise. Never again.

That afternoon, Tere left the manager's office exhausted, but relieved. Amparito picked them up sooner than agreed, and they all rode home in silence. When Tere's mom asked her if she'd had a good time at the mall, Tere said it was okay.

Tere and Conchita never spoke about what had happened that Saturday. They remained friendly, but something had changed forever. Tere now knew to follow her heart before anyone else's. She might not be popular and crazy, but she could be strong under pressure. She could be true to herself.

And, from then on, she was.

The Magician's Granddaughter

by Janette Rallison

My best friend, Priscilla, opened the door to our spare bedroom and stepped inside. "Come on, Faith. You won't get in trouble. It will be our secret."

I followed her, looking at Grandpa's things stacked up in the corner of the room. It all smelled very Grandpa-y inside, even though he'd only been at our house for two days. Exactly where does that smell come from?

"We'll just stay for a minute," I said. Grandpa had left with my parents to go out to dinner so it wasn't likely any of them would hear us, but I whispered, anyway. They didn't take me to dinner, by the way, because I had to babysit Arianna, my five-year-old sister. Arianna doesn't do well at restaurants. Last time she went to one, she spent half of dinner leaning over our booth talking to the people behind us. Which might not have been so bad if she hadn't spilled her soda on them, too.

So my parents decided to leave her home. Arianna was now perched in front of the TV watching a video while Priscilla and I invaded the guest bedroom.

I know what you're thinking. Why would any self-respecting twelve-year-old even care what was in her grandpa's suitcases? If you went through your average grandpa's travel bag, you'd just find a bunch of rolled-up socks and a bottle of aspirin. But my grandfather is Jaramino the Magnificent. He travels around California doing magic shows. When he has a show in Los Angeles, he always stays with us, and we all get to see him for free. Even Arianna, who doesn't quite understand the whole concept of magic. I mean, I've convinced her I can change stoplights from red to green by waving my hands at them and chanting, "Obey me, insignificant traffic light!" Arianna just goes because she likes seeing him turn a stuffed animal into a rabbit. It's her favorite trick.

As I thought of this, I realized something for the first time. Grandpa has a rabbit in his act, and yet all the times he's stayed with us I've never seen the rabbit. Shouldn't he have a cage for it? I looked around at the cases in the room. None of them looked like something an animal could live in.

Priscilla flipped open a small box that sat on larger ones. "It's makeup," she said with surprise. "Your grandpa wears makeup?"

"Everyone wears makeup onstage," I said. "Otherwise, the lights wash you out, and you look pale and sickly."

Priscilla set the case down with a thud. "Well, where does he keep the good stuff? You know, those rings that no one can ever get apart or the huge scarves he pulls out of a little box?"

I walked to a large trunk at the end of the bed and opened it. Inside were not only the rings and the scarves, but the empty pitcher that kept pouring water, the red Styrofoam balls that would appear and disappear in different places all through Grandpa's show, and the plush white stuffed rabbit.

Priscilla got out two huge silver rings and examined them. "I don't see any holes in these. How does he get them together?"

"I don't know. He won't tell me." And, believe me, it wasn't for lack of trying on my part. I've always wanted to be a magician, too, but whenever I ask Grandpa how he does things, he says, "A magician never reveals his secrets." Or he gives me some long story about how he traveled through the jungles of

Peru and picked up magic potions from some long lost tribe. Yeah, right. Only Arianna believes that.

I can keep a secret. Why doesn't he see that?

Priscilla put down the rings and opened up another box. "Maybe if we keep looking through his stuff, it will give us some clue how it works."

"We have to put everything back exactly where we found it. If he finds out we've snooped in his things, he'll kill us." I had visions, just then, of Grandpa using me for the sawing-the-lady-in-half trick.

"Right." Priscilla opened another box and peered inside. "We'll be careful."

We shuffled through Grandpa's stuff for another ten minutes, handling objects like sacred relics. I found a bottle marked MAGIC POWDER. He sprinkled that on the toy rabbit to turn it into a real one. I opened the bottle and examined the white sparkly powder. It looked like glitter.

"Hey, here's a book." Priscilla lifted up a banged-up journal with the word *Peru* written in ink across the front. "Maybe it tells how to do some of the tricks."

"He wouldn't carry around a book that tells him how to do his own tricks. He already knows how. Besides, I'm sure he never went to Peru."

Priscilla ignored me and kept reading. "He wrote in here that he translated all this from Quechua. What's that?"

"Some language he made up. He says that's what they speak in the jungles of Peru, but everybody knows they speak Spanish. It's listed on the map at school as a Spanish-speaking country."

Priscilla flipped through more pages. "Wow, here's the rabbit trick."

I walked over to where she sat and peered over her shoulder. On the page was a drawing of a rabbit plus the instructions: *Sprinkle thoroughly and cover object with cloth. Transformation may take up to one minute.*

"That doesn't tell how to do the trick," I said. "Where does the real rabbit come from?"

Priscilla didn't answer. Just then, the bedroom door opened. She dropped the book as though it had caught on fire, and we both spun around.

Arianna stood in the doorway. "What are you doing in Grandpa's room?"

"Nothing," I said.

Arianna tilted her head at me. "You're not supposed to touch Grandpa's things. I'm telling."

I smiled at her and used my I'm-a-nice-big-sister voice. "We're not getting into Grandpa's things. We're just cleaning up for him." I picked up the notebook and placed it back in the trunk. "See. Cleaning."

She shook her head. "Grandpa's going to be real mad. He'll probably turn you into a puppy or something."

"People don't turn into other things." Unless you counted my parents, who would both turn into something totally frightening when they found out what I'd done. I bent down to be on Arianna's level. "We'll show you a magic trick if you promise not to tell."

Her face brightened. "Okay. Show me the rabbit one." She hopped onto the bed, waiting expectantly.

I turned to Priscilla. "I'll take Arianna into my room and show her the rabbit trick. You clean up in here. When everything is put back right, come tell me."

I grabbed the stuffed rabbit, the bottle of magic glitter, and Arianna's hand; then we walked down the hall to my bedroom. Once there, Arianna climbed on my bed and watched me place the rabbit on my dresser. I took a bandanna out of my drawer to cover the stuffed animal.

"It might not work the first time," I told her. "I might have to try it a bunch of times." At least until Priscilla showed up, and we were free and clear of getting in trouble.

I unscrewed the bottle of glitter and was glad I'd thought to come to my room. After all, if Grandpa found glitter sprinkled on his carpet, he would know what we'd done.

I took a pinch of the magic powder, said, "Hocus

Pocus"—and with a flourish threw it toward the rabbit. This was my first mistake. The powder was lighter than I'd thought and, with the help of my ceiling fan, a glitter cloud swooshed across my bedroom. I would be dusting that stuff off for the next week.

I laid the bandanna over the rabbit and stalled. "It takes a while," I said.

"Grandpa always tells jokes at this part," Arianna told me.

"Right—jokes." That would keep her busy for a while. I told her a couple of knock-knock jokes that she probably didn't get but she laughed, anyway. Then she jumped off the bed, squealed, "It worked!" and grabbed my bandanna off the stuffed animal. Only it wasn't a stuffed animal anymore. It was a fat, furry, nose-scrunching rabbit.

I stared at it with my mouth hanging open. "That's impossible."

Arianna picked up the rabbit and held it close to her. "I'm going to name you Bob."

"Priscilla!" I yelled. "Priscilla, come here!"

A minute later, Priscilla opened the door. "Hold your horses. I couldn't remember where the scarves went and—hey, you got the rabbit trick to work. How'd you do that?"

I waved my hand in the direction of Arianna and

the rabbit. "I didn't. I mean, I just sprinkled the magic powder on the rabbit, and it happened all by itself."

Priscilla lifted one eyebrow like she thought I was lying. "Right. If you don't want to tell me, that's—" She stopped speaking, tilted her head, and stepped toward my bed. "What happened to your stuffed animals?"

I have two stuffed animals that I keep by my pillow. A tiger I've had since I was little, and a unicorn I won at the state fair last year. Neither was there. In their place, a miniature tiger hissed and growled at a small unicorn. The unicorn kept lunging toward the tiger, trying to stab the cat with its horn.

I picked up the unicorn. "Hey, stop that!"

Okay—maybe it's not a good idea to grab an angry unicorn, even if it is only a foot long. But after all, I did own it; and it had spent every night for the last year on my bed, so you would think it would show me some respect. But—no. It promptly tried to gore my arm until I sat it down on the floor. Then it threw its mane back in a disgusted manner and trotted underneath my bed.

Arianna put the rabbit down on my bed and picked up the tiger. "Poor kitty. I'm going to name you Candy Cane, because you're striped."

I took the tiger from her hands. "You can't hold that. It's a tiger."

Arianna leaned over and scratched the cat's chin. "It's a nice tiger, though. Aren't you, Candy Cane?"

The tiger purred momentarily, then caught sight of the rabbit. I could feel its claws digging into my chest as it tried to push away from me. I hurried to my closet, threw the tiger inside, and leaned against the door. Priscilla watched all of this with her jaw hanging slackly.

"We have to find a way to turn them all back," I told her. "Go get Grandpa's book."

She nodded and fled the room.

The tiger let out angry growls from the closet. One paw shot out from underneath the door and nearly clawed my feet. I jumped away with a shriek, which spooked the rabbit, so that it leaped from my quilt and hopped underneath the bed. The unicorn let out a whinny. Apparently it wasn't happy to have its territory invaded by a giant rabbit—but I wasn't worried about that right now.

Movement on my bookshelf caught my eye. My Chinese glass dragon had transformed into a large, pacing lizard that kept blowing clouds of smoke onto the books behind it.

Okay, that was probably bad.

Priscilla opened my door and breathlessly handed me Grandpa's journal. I sat on my bed, opened it, and tried to find the rabbit trick again. Where was it?

The rabbit darted out from underneath my bed with the unicorn close behind. They ran through Arianna's legs, and circled the room several times until the rabbit finally smashed itself behind my dresser. The unicorn stomped its feet, held its head up, and trotted back underneath my bed.

"I thought unicorns were supposed to be nice creatures," Priscilla said. "You know, friendly and stuff."

I flipped through a few pages. "We'll change them back, and then everything will be normal again." Just as I said this, the dragon set one of my books on fire. Priscilla beat out the flames with my pillow while I continued to look for the rabbit-trick instructions. It had been toward the front of the book, hadn't it?

"You're a nice dragon," I heard Arianna say. "I'll name you Flame."

"Don't touch the dragon," I said without looking up. "Priscilla, don't let her touch anything that moves."

I turned another page. There in front of me lay the instructions for the rabbit trick. I wanted to cry with relief.

"Uh, Faith, I think you should see this." The tone

of Priscilla's voice left me no option. I looked. She pointed to the top shelf of my bookcase.

Back when I was eight and played with Barbies, my mother bought me an expensive, collectible princess-doll series. They're up high on the shelf to keep Arianna from touching them. Now they were all pushing off the lids of their boxes.

I jumped up from the bed and rushed over to my bookshelf. "Excuse me, you can't do that. You can't get out of your boxes because then you'll lose your value. You're NRFB. That means never removed from box, so if you don't mind—"

The Rapunzel doll let out a cough and heaved herself onto the shelf. "Do you ever dust up here? Look at this. It's so thick you could make dust angels."

"Back in the box," I told her.

The Cinderella and Snow White dolls emerged, shaking their hair like models in shampoo commercials. "Who's that?" Cinderella asked Snow White.

Snow White glanced at me and shrugged. "I've never seen her. She looks like a wicked stepmother, though."

I put my hands on my hips. "I beg your pardon. I *own* you."

"Yep," Cinderella said. "Definitely a wicked stepmother."

Next to me, Arianna clapped her hands. "They're pretty. Can I play with them?"

"No," I said.

Sleeping Beauty stretched and looked over the shelf at us. "I'm starving. A proper hostess would serve us some food."

"Sorry. I'm a little busy right now," I said.

Snow White walked over to Sleeping Beauty, swishing her dress as she went. "I come with an apple. It's too bad you only come with a doll stand."

Sleeping Beauty then picked up her doll stand and smacked the apple out of Snow White's hand. "Doll stands come in handy if you know how to use them."

Snow White yelled out several things, none of which you'd expect to hear from a fairy-tale princess. Meanwhile, Sleeping Beauty triumphantly picked up the apple, took a bite, and fell down on the shelf.

Priscilla gasped and turned to me. "She just ate the—shouldn't we do something?"

"She's Sleeping Beauty. She's supposed to be asleep. What do you want me to do, find a bunch of dwarfs to take care of her?"

The dolls were all out of their boxes and strolling around the shelf, which was definitely some sort of collectible tragedy; but short of picking them up and shoving them back inside their containers, there was nothing I could do. I had to let them stay up there until I figured out how to turn them back into harmless plastic figurines. I sat back down on my bed and picked up the book again. "Priscilla, can you keep an eye on them while I read this?"

"All right." Priscilla took a step toward my bookcase.

Cinderella turned to Rapunzel. "She sent an ugly stepsister to watch us."

"Hey," Priscilla said. "I resent that."

Cinderella nodded sadly. "Of course, you do, Ugly Dear. You must resent your looks quite a bit."

All the dolls snickered at this.

Priscilla shook her head. "And to think I used to feel sorry for Cinderella. Why don't you make yourself useful and clean up all that dust up there. Stepsister's orders."

Cinderella raised her chin and folded her arms. "I don't have to listen to you. My prince will save me. And when he does, he'll chop off your big, ugly head."

Priscilla shot me a look.

"Don't worry," I said. "No princes came with the collection."

I was trying to concentrate on the words in front of me, but it was hard to do with all of the shelf drama going on.

"This is what I did to escape from my tower," Rapunzel said. I glanced up and saw her lying down on the shelf as she tossed her long, braided hair over the edge. "Any moment now, a prince will come along and—oh, I feel something. It's a . . . It's a . . . Ahhh! There's a huge lizard on my hair! Get it off!"

The dragon was clinging to Rapunzel's hair. She wildly swung around in an attempt to shake it off. The lizard snorted angrily at her hair, leaving big sooty circles on it.

This was so killing my doll's resale value.

I glued my gaze back to the book. And then I saw it, scrawled at the bottom of the next page: *Use restoring dust to undo the trick.*

"Priscilla, we've got to go back to Grandpa's room and find the restoring dust."

Her eyebrows scrunched together, and she shook her head. "There wasn't any restoring dust. I looked at everything. I would have remembered it."

And then, I heard the garage door open. "They're home," I whispered. "What are we going to do?"

Priscilla had grabbed the dragon by its sides to extract it from Rapunzel's hair, but it shot a tiny flame at her and she dropped it to the floor. The dragon hissed at us and ran under the bed. Two seconds later, it ran back out, followed by a charging unicorn.

"Maybe no one will notice," Priscilla said.

"My dolls are trying to rappel down the bookcase. I have a tiger in my closet and a unicorn that keeps chasing animals around my room. I *think* my parents will notice."

Priscilla stepped out of the way of the speeding unicorn. "You know, it's time for me to go home."

I spread my hands out at the chaos my room had become. "What am I supposed to do with all this stuff?"

She shrugged. "You could use them for your school science project. I bet you'd get an A."

A knock sounded on my door, and my mother's voice said, "We're home. Is everything all right?"

Priscilla and I looked at each other but didn't answer.

"We're having fun!" Arianna shouted. "Faith's doing magic."

"That's nice," Mom called back, and her footsteps receded.

"Sorry, but I've really got to leave." Priscilla walked to the door and gave me an apologetic look. "I don't want to be around when your grandfather finds out what happened. He might turn me into something scary." Without another word, she slipped out the door.

I looked around my room again and felt tears

pressing against the back of my eyes. I didn't want to be a magician anymore. In fact, I never wanted to see another trick again. Why in the world had I gotten into Grandpa's stuff? I took Arianna by the hand and led her out of the room. "Go watch TV while I talk to Grandpa."

Arianna can smell trouble. She skipped off to the family room without argument. I went and knocked on Grandpa's door.

"Come in," he called.

I stepped inside. He was sitting on the bed, taking off his shoes.

"Um," I said, and couldn't say anything else for a moment. I watched him loosen his shoelaces while I tried to force words from my mouth. "So, you know how you've always told me never to touch your stuff?"

He looked up, a shoe in his hand. "Yes."

"Well, I did. I got into your stuff because I wanted to see how it worked. And then Arianna came in, so I told her I'd do a trick for her if she didn't tell on me."

His bushy eyebrows drew together. "Did you break something?"

"No. But I used the magic powder, and now there's a unicorn running around my room, a dragon is under my bed, all of my dolls are out of their boxes, and your rabbit is hiding behind my dresser. I'm *really* sorry, Grandpa."

He put his shoe down on the floor as though it was perfectly normal to hear all this. "Now you know why you shouldn't go poking into other people's things," he said.

I looked down at the floor. "I'm sorry, but you never told me it was real magic."

"I've always told you it was real magic. You just haven't believed me in a long time."

Which was true, of course, but who could blame me?

His other shoe fell to the floor with a thud. "The world is full of magic. You just have to know where to look, where not to look, and when to duck."

I glanced back up at Grandpa. "I want you to tell me everything about magic, but, well, first could you tell me where to get some restoring dust? You see, the little dragon might start a fire in my bookcase again."

Grandpa picked up his shoes, walked to the closet, and dropped them inside. "You've already used it."

"But I never saw it. I only took the magic powder."

"Truth is the restoring powder." Grandpa picked up his slippers and slid his feet into them. "Powerful magic, that's what truth is. You told me what happened, so when you go back to your room, you'll find that everything has been restored."

I didn't wait for him to say any more. I darted out of his room and into mine. My stuffed animals lay on the bed. The glass dragon sat perched upon my bookshelf. Every doll stood smiling in her box. Grandpa's bunny was back on the dresser, right where it had been before I did the trick.

I picked up the rabbit and the bottle of magic powder, then jogged back to Grandpa's room. I handed him both. "It worked," I said.

Grandpa smiled. He placed the rabbit and the bottle back into their boxes.

"How do you turn the rabbit back during your shows?" I asked.

"After every performance, I tell the audience I'm glad they came to watch me perform magic, trickery, and pure nonsense. It's the truth every time I say it."

"Oh." I watched him close the lids of the trunks and felt relieved that the magic was locked up. "Sorry, again."

"No harm done and you've realized something, too. That's a good day in my way of thinking."

I stood there a moment longer. "Are you going to tell my parents about this?"

"You think they'd be mad at you?"

I let out a snort. "Yeah!"

"Oh, I don't think your mother could be very mad." He smiled and walked back over to me. "Can you keep a secret?"

I nodded.

"When your mother was your age, she did the very same thing. Turned a bear, a hippopotamus, and four monkeys to life. Worse yet, she didn't tell me for two days. By that time, they'd nearly torn the house apart."

"Mom did that? *My* mother?"

Grandpa laughed. "Magic runs strong in our family—but that's our secret, too."

The Green Pail

by Coleen Murtagh Paratore

Somehow the green pail caught my eye as we left our camp that day.

Summer was over. We were going home. School was starting Monday.

I was twelve, nearly thirteen, and wedged sweaty between mountains of dirty laundry and three fidgeting brothers in the back of the station wagon, my stomach was already mixing its September recipe. One cup, excited; two cups, dread.

But what was that green pail doing there?

We had cleaned up the yard so thoroughly. Mom and I did the inside earlier. Shelves emptied, floors swept, mousetraps set. Outside, we stored our toys in the shed, my bike always last and hardest to part with. The tires spun as my father slammed the door, hitched the lock, and stuffed the key in his pocket.

Our summer camp was officially closed. Not a blade of grass was out of place.

That's why I was so surprised to see the green pail, sitting on the step in front of the shed. It was just an ordinary little plastic pail, the kind I used to make sand castles with. For some reason, though, it seemed important. I strained my ears to listen.

Silly, I know, green pails don't talk. Did anyone else notice it?

I looked quickly at my father, my mother, my brothers. No, they didn't see.

"Say, 'Good-bye, camp,'" Mom instructs, this year with less spark in her voice.

"Good-bye," we call in chorus, like the good children we are.

My father hits the gas, gravel crunches, and we pull out of the driveway. Inside my head I whisper, *Good-bye, green pail, good-bye*.

I crane my neck to keep it in view. It shrinks small as a leaf, then it's gone, and now I begin to worry. It seemed so lonely sitting there. What if the wind blows it away? Or a raccoon chews its handle off? Or it fills with snow and freezes . . .

"Wake up, Annie," my father shouts. "Can't you hear your brother screaming?"

"Sorry." I screw the top off Jackie's bottle, *sniff*, not too sour, and stick it in his mouth. He hiccups, wraps his hand around my finger, watching me with grateful eyes.

Up front, Mom sighs and leans her head against the window—closed, though it must be ninety degrees. She doesn't say anything. She doesn't turn around. She's fat with another "little one" coming. That's what they call them, the "little ones."

Eddie is five. Danny's three. Jackie's almost one.

I'll be thirteen soon. I'm excited, but more excited about my friend Maggie's birthday. She's having a party next Saturday night. Her mother said boys can come. Mag's inviting Johnny Keating for her and Billy Finelly for me. I hope I'm brave enough to talk to him.

It's late when I crawl into bed, aching from all the unpacking. My window's open, begging for a breeze. I hear cars zooming past outside, Mom mumbling, Dad shouting . . .

My summer life is so much nicer. Mom and us kids stay at our camp on Loon Lake. My father only comes out on the weekends. I still have to help with the little ones, but when my father's away, it's not so strict. I don't feel like a loon in a cage.

Jackie starts crying. Dad shouts again. I scratch the wall.

Nine months until I am free again, fish diving to the bottom of the lake and up, sailing dirt roads on my bike, singing wildly, wind whistling, wildflowers in my basket, breathing pine, giggling with my summer friends, spying on the boy next door.

I can't have a bike here in the city. I can't leave the yard except for school. When I get home, I have to babysit, and then there's dinner and dishes and hours of homework and my father is always watching.

I dig out my diary, turn on my light, and write. *Billy Finelly sat with me on the bus the last day of school. I had to press my books down to keep my legs from shaking. Billy has sweet-sad cow-brown eyes and dark, curly hair. Patty Haight, sounds like "hate," kept staring at us. Patty Haight likes Billy, too. She already hates me because of Maggie. She wants Mag to be her best friend . . .* On and on and on I write.

When I'm writing, I feel like I'm riding my bike or fish diving deep.

When I close my eyes to sleep, I see the green pail sitting there.

The first day of eighth grade isn't too bad. Except for Math A. I was supposed to be in Math B, but my father made them move me to the advanced class. My father didn't go to college. He wants to make sure I do.

Billy Finelly sits with me on the bus. *Say something, Annie, come on.*

"Are you going to Maggie's party?" he asks.

I nod. Billy smiles and I smile, too. I feel Patty Haight's hate on my back.

I'm so excited, I nearly leap off the bus. Then I walk inside and fear freezes me.

My father is standing by my bedroom door with my diary in his hand.

"Who's this Billy boy?" he says.

"Nobody." My face is burning. *You had no right to read my diary.*

Little Danny wraps his arms around my legs. "I miss you, Annie. Come play."

"Do your homework," my father says. He tosses my diary on the table.

I am a mannequin moving. Dinner, dishes, homework. Then I open my diary and start ripping. *Ripping, ripping, ripping* . . . I rip my secrets into white and ink-blue confetti and plunge them in the garbage can.

I plan my outfit for the party. My favorite jeans, yellow top, hair parted differently. Earrings, makeup . . . a bit more. *Hello, Billy . . . Hi, Bill . . . Hey, Bill, how's it going?* I practice so I won't sound stupid.

* * *

The phone rings. My father answers it. "That's awful," he says. "Tell your daughter we're sorry. I'll handle this right now." He slams down the receiver. "What's wrong with you, Annie? Making fun of that girl's scars."

My mind is swirling. *What's he talking about?* "No, Dad, I didn't. I swear—"

"Don't swear at me. She told her mother you laughed at the scars on her leg."

Patty Haight. She has ugly scars on her leg from a bike accident, but I would never laugh at that. "It's not true, Dad, please believe me."

"Why would Ellen Haight's daughter lie?"

"I don't know, Dad, but I'm *your daughter*," I shriek too loudly.

"Don't shout at me," he says. Eddie starts crying, and then baby Jackie.

"Bad Daddy," Danny says. "No Annie boo-boo." He kicks my father.

"*Shhh*, Danny," I say, "it's okay."

"You're grounded," my father says and storms out the door.

I lay in bed, aching to write it all down. That's the only way I know to keep from drowning. To write through the pain to the shore. I cry and cry and cry. I can't breathe.

And then I see it.

The green pail. Sitting there by the shed.

And I pick it up and I fill it.

I fill it with pain and rage and fear and words and words and words.

"You have to come, Annie," Maggie says.

"No, Mag. He'll never let me out."

"Get your mother to help," Maggie says. "Can't she do something for once?"

"Please, Mom. I just want to go to Maggie's party. She's my best . . ."

Uh-huhhhhhhhhhh. My mother sighs and rubs her back. She tears open the box and dumps in the noodles. Water sputters and steam rises. Her hair hangs limp around her face, eyes closed like she's in a sauna. Then so softly I'm not sure if it's her or the water boiling she says, "I'll think of a way."

"Thank you." I hug her tight, careful not to squish the new little one.

It's Saturday at five o'clock. The party is at seven.

Mom makes the little ones English muffin pizzas with pepperoni faces. She gives them warm bubble baths.

I read them stories, and they fall asleep peaceful as angels at six.

Mom cooks my father a huge sirloin steak, gravy, mushrooms, baked potatoes with sour cream. She brings it to the living room where he's watching a game. He eats and lies back on the couch. Soon we hear the snoring.

Mom flicks the TV off and on to check. We smile. He's out for the night.

Mom comes in my room as I'm fixing my hair. She has two pillows in her hands.

"You look pretty," she says.

Mom shapes the pillows to look like a girl fast asleep in her bed. "I'm sorry, Annie, for all of it." She kisses me on the cheek. "Tonight be a princess, baby."

It's dark outside and I run.

Maggie's house is warm with friends. Balloons and streamers, music blasting. Baked macaroni, hot dogs in pastry. Ginger ale fizzing with maraschino cherries.

Maggie is dancing, but I'm too nervous. Billy is watching me.

We sing "Happy Birthday." Mag cuts her cake. She opens her presents. I check the clock. *Come on, Annie, go talk to him.*

"We've got games in the basement," Mag says. "Come on, everybody."

My legs are cookies crumbling down the stairs.

It's dark and cooler here. I have to leave soon. My heart is pounding. I close my eyes.

The green pail is there.

Billy is leaning on the ping-pong table. I walk over. "Hey, Billy, want to play?"

"Sure."

I've never played ping-pong in my life, but tonight somehow I do.

"You're good," he says.

"Thanks. You, too."

"How long have you been playing?" Billy says.

"One night."

He laughs and I laugh and I run home laughing, before the clock strikes ten.

That night, I lie awake remembering. Billy and the ping-pong game.

I fill the green pail to the top.

Then I pour it safely into my heart, ready to fill again.

The Royal Clue

by Jaclyn Moriarty

The following story takes place in a far-off Kingdom. There is little documentary proof that this Kingdom even exists. In my opinion, however, it does. It is also my opinion that the Kingdom has a serious problem with certain of its schoolteachers. I have no doubt that the teachers in your own Kingdom are nothing like these teachers. If they are, I suggest you notify your principal.

The first time Lucy saw the Royal Clue, she was on her way to school.

The Clue was in the playground. Huge silver letters hung suspended from the top bar of the jungle gym. Small children were climbing on the letters. Nearby, mothers chatted. Lucy stopped and pulled at her coat sleeves.

"Hey! Get those children off there!"

A man in a suit was tumbling out of a car. He sprinted across the playground, waving his hands at the children. The mothers turned slowly.

"Can't you see?" shouted the man. He was already lifting the children down from the letters. "Can't you see that *this* is the Royal Clue?"

The silver letters shivered in the breeze. The letters spelled a word: SECRETS.

Lucy saw the Clue twice more before she got to school. Blocky silver letters on the roof of the ice-cream parlor. SECRETS, said the letters. The same letters lying flat in the sandpit at the nursery school. SECRETS, they said, and they were spangled with frost.

Lucy stared at the sandbox until her face burned with the cold.

Even then, she did not hurry, but dawdled toward school.

At her classroom door, she slowly reached for the handle.

But the door was thrown open with a shout. "Lucy Gold! I *completely forgot* you existed! I was *so* happy! And now it appears you *do* exist. Look at me! I am *so* sad!"

A tall man in a purple cloak stood at the classroom door. He pulled a tragic face and stepped aside.

This was Lucy's teacher.

Mr. Turnpike.

"I'm sorry I'm late," Lucy whispered.

But Mr. Turnpike leaped into the air. "You are *fifteen* minutes late and you are *sorry*? Class, what should we do about her?!"

The class shrugged uncomfortably. They did not know what to do about Mr. Turnpike.

He had never taken to Lucy.

"Excuse me," he had frowned at her on the first day of school. "Did you know there are *holes* in the elbows of your sweater?"

Lucy had made a mistake. She thought he was joking.

"But, Mr. Turnpike," she smiled. "You have holes in your jeans."

The class giggled. They also thought Mr. Turnpike was joking. Everyone stared at the holes in the knees of Mr. Turnpike's jeans.

"These?" breathed Mr. Turnpike, bending to look at his knees. *"These!?"* Now his eyes were popping. "These are *designer* holes! They're *frayed* just so! I paid *countless* fortunes to buy these jeans! And you *dare* to *compare* them to the worn-out holes in your sweater!? What have you done with your *manners*?"

He spent the rest of the day teaching the class about designer brands.

On the second day of school, Mr. Turnpike had instructed his class to bring in their parents' income-tax returns from the previous year.

On the third day of school, Mr. Turnpike read through the income-tax returns. He nodded, pleased. "I don't really like children," he confided to the class. "But you have wealthy mommies and daddies!" He smiled around at the class. "They all make lots of money, and that makes you easier to teach!"

Then he got to Lucy's father. Everyone knew it must be Lucy's father because he looked at Lucy, then down at the paper, up and down, up and down, his face turning the color of fog.

"Your father makes no money at *all*?" he breathed.

"He's sick," explained Lucy. "He has the coughing sickness."

"What about your mother?" Mr. Turnpike said hopefully.

"She died when I was a baby."

"So this is it?" Mr. Turnpike said. "Your family has no money?"

Lucy nodded.

"Well, *this* is the absolute *limit*! A *child* as *poor* as *this*! She must be the poorest in the Kingdom! I will not have it! I will *not*!"

The class thought he might plan a cookie drive to raise money for Lucy's family.

They still didn't know Mr. Turnpike.

He stamped his foot like an angry horse. "I cannot teach a child this poor! I *refuse*! I'm going to see the principal!"

He stormed out of the classroom. Lucy bit her lip. Mr. Turnpike returned.

"It seems that *poverty* is not a reason to get a student expelled! Can you believe it, class? That awful principal won't even let me transfer her to another grade!" He began to mutter. "And I'm allergic to poor people! My doctor tells me I should never even *look* at them! And if I *do* look at them, I'm supposed to imagine them as very, very small." Now he squinted at Lucy. "All right, you're getting smaller." He began to smile. "Why, you are so tiny, I can hardly *see* you! Oh, you have a desk, I see!" He giggled. "Get up, child! You don't need a desk! You can fit between the cracks in the floorboards!"

And that was the start of Mr. Turnpike's in-between game.

But on this cold morning, Mr. Turnpike was in a state again.

"By being late, you remind me of your regular size," he explained reasonably. "And I was doing such a good job of making you teeny-tiny in my mind! My allergies were getting so much better! So, that is cruel. Also, you weren't here this morning, which means you *abandoned* me! How would *you* feel if I abandoned *you* for fifteen minutes!"

The class shifted. This made no sense.

"If you don't want to see her," began one brave boy, "how can you say she *abandons* you when she's . . ."

But Mr. Turnpike was staring through the classroom window.

"What's that?" he murmured. "On the bench there? Is that—do my eyes deceive me? *Is that a Royal Clue?*"

And in a sudden gust of cloak and door, he was gone.

The class turned to the window.

There was Mr. Turnpike galloping across the asphalt toward a wooden bench. Pressed into the seat of that bench: enormous silver letters. The letters glinted in the cold sunlight. SECRETS, they said to the class.

Mr. Turnpike stayed on the bench for the rest of the day. He studied the silver letters with a magnifying glass.

At first, Lucy's classmates talked among themselves, now and then looking through the window to check on Mr. Turnpike. They relaxed. Children put their feet up on desks.

But the principal, hearing the chatter, came to check on them.

"Hmm," she said, watching Mr. Turnpike through the window. "I suppose we'll let him look at the Clue for a bit. It *is* very important. Does everybody know why it's important?"

Of course, everybody knew! It was the Royal Clue!

Nevertheless, the principal explained.

"Once a year," she said, "the royal family tours the Kingdom. Nobody knows where the tour will go. But if a Royal Clue appears in a town, it means that town has been chosen. The family will arrive in a fortnight!

"In that fortnight," the principal continued, "the most talented people in town try to solve the Royal Clue. Whoever solves the Clue wins the prize! And aren't you lucky, children, that your teacher is so talented? *He* might win the prize!"

She pointed through the window at Mr. Turnpike. He was kneeling up on the bench now, his bottom in the air. He seemed to be sniffing at the letters.

Hmm, the principal murmured to herself. She instructed the class to watch movies and play cards.

Walking home from school that day, Lucy saw that her town was alight with excitement. There was running, skipping, and shouting. People came out of their houses in pajamas, their arms folded tightly for warmth while they chatted with strangers. A group of builders marched by Lucy, planks of wood on their shoulders. "That's for the royal stadium!" shouted a man in mittens.

Meanwhile, the Royal Clue had appeared in three more places: Lucy saw the silver SECRETS in the window of the candy shop, in flashing lights at the video arcade, and in spray paint in the skateboard park. (Some teenagers appeared with SECRETS shaved into their hair, but it turned out they'd done that themselves.)

Already, crowds of talented people had gathered around each of the Clues. Scientists were scraping up samples from the letters, ready to send to their labs. Philosophers were squinting and nodding. Professors of literature flicked through books, highlighting the word *secrets* wherever it appeared. Photographers photographed the letters. Psychologists questioned them. Podiatrists studied their feet.

By the time she got home, Lucy was bursting with hope. Mr. Turnpike would get caught up in this fever! He might be away from school for *weeks*.

But the next day, he was back. The principal had told him he could only look at the Clue in the afternoons and should never sniff at it.

Mr. Turnpike cheered himself up by teasing Lucy. It also helped his allergies to make fun of poor people.

"Oh," he said to Lucy. "I accidentally saw your *house* the other day! It's so *ramshackle*! Are you sure it's not a dog kennel?"

Or else, "I was reading this morning that you can cure the coughing sickness by taking maple candy in the southern climes. I can't *think* why your father doesn't go there. Could it be—of course! He can't afford the airfare! Ah, well. Never mind."

And so on.

Mostly, though, he liked to play the in-between game.

The game was simple. Mr. Turnpike would tell the class to stand in a circle with their arms linked. Lucy had to stay seated while her classmates did this. Then he would exclaim, "Oh, there's that teeny-tiny girl. Well, she can fit *in between* somewhere. Go on, in-between girl, join the circle."

Lucy would try to join the circle but, of course, her classmates' arms were linked. Now and then, someone would unlink arms, to let her in, but the teacher always spotted that. "CHEATING! STOP IT! SHE MUST FIND HER WAY *IN BETWEEN*!"

Mr. Turnpike laughed happily while Lucy walked around the circle. Eventually, he grew bored and told everyone to sit down.

Or else, he would take Lucy's chair, turn it upside down, and say, "Hey, in-between girl, why the chair? You can fit between the doormat and the floor!"

Or, he would make himself a cup of tea and hold up the sugar bowl. "In-between girl!" he would call. "Come see if you can fit between the crystals in this sugar bowl!" He would pour his tea right into the bowl. "See that! The *tea* found a way to fit between the sugar. Why not you?"

Sometimes, Mr. Turnpike stopped mid-sentence and cried, "Class! Why waste my time? I'm trying to solve the Royal Clue!" Then he told them to listen to their iPods, and sat with his eyes closed and his head in his hands.

Meanwhile, the town was in a frenzy. There was just one week until the royal family arrived. The stadium was not ready! The royal cheesecake was not baked! And, most important of all, the talented people had not yet solved the Clue!

Some said they *had* solved the Clue. They were very annoying about it, holding up their notebooks and saying, "The answer's right here!" before stuffing the notebooks in their pockets and running away. Others chased them, bribed them, and blackmailed them. Once, a notebook was stolen, and word got around that its owner thought the answer to the Clue was this: "Send Every Cat 'Round Every Tree (Sorry!)"

Everyone laughed at this, and went back to the Clues. They slept in tents beside the Clues. They poured chemicals over the letters. They chanted, stared, and frowned.

They frowned most deeply when children were nearby, affecting their concentration. Of course, the Royal Clue had appeared in places where children played—playground, ice-cream parlor, nursery school, school yard, candy shop, video arcade, and skateboard park—so children were often nearby. Whenever they got too close, the talented people stamped and clapped their hands, as if the children were seagulls.

At last, the day of the royal visit arrived.

Lucy woke before dawn. She knew she should try to sleep again, but her father was snoring loudly across the room.

So she lay in bed and thought about Mr. Turnpike. Perhaps he would solve the Clue today? He would win the prize and never be a teacher again.

She would never have to play the in-between game again.

An icy breeze found its way between the cracks in the cottage walls. Lucy tried to fall asleep in the space between her father's snores.

In the end, she got up. She was sleepy and confused.

The oatmeal was almost empty. *That's all right*, she thought. *I can eat the spaces in between the oatmeal.* She put the oatmeal back on the shelf.

She reached for the front door handle and thought, *But why open the door? I can fit in the space between the door and its frame.*

She stared at the door for a moment, then opened it.

Outside, it was raining, but Lucy did not have an umbrella.

That's all right, she thought, *I can fit between the raindrops and stay dry.*

By the time she arrived at school, she was drenched.

Mr. Turnpike did not notice. He was too excited. He was dressed in his best purple cloak and had dyed his hair orange and spiked it.

"Today," he told the class, "I will win the royal prize! I have *solved* the Royal Clue!" He danced around the desks and clapped his hands.

The class was also excited. At 10 A.M., the whole school would march to the stadium, to watch the royal tour. There would be fireworks and a feast.

But at 9:45 A.M., Mr. Turnpike exclaimed, "I can't *stand* the suspense! Come on, class! Let's run to the stadium now! We'll get the best seats!"

He threw open the classroom door, and the class began to pour out of the room.

"Oh, help!" Mr. Turnpike gasped suddenly. "I'm supposed to tidy the classroom before I leave. In case the royal family wants to tour the school! But if I don't go now, I'll miss the best seats!" He spied Lucy, just outside the classroom door. "Perfect! The in-between girl! You stay and tidy up. Don't worry about being late! You can fit *between* the best seats!"

Some of Lucy's classmates hesitated, looking at Lucy with troubled frowns. Mr. Turnpike's game had surely gone too far? But he hurried them out of the classroom, slamming the door behind him.

He had already put the door on automatic lock. There was a clunking sound.

Lucy stared at the handle for a moment. She tried to open it. Nothing. She watched through the window as children hurried across the school grounds. Mr. Turnpike sprinted along, soon overtaking his class.

Slowly, she tidied the room, now and then glancing at the door.

But each time she tried it, it was locked.

She looked up at the air vents in the ceiling.

She could fit between the vents! She could escape!

Half an hour later, she was sitting at her desk, still staring at the vents, when she heard a sound like a distant lion roaring. That was the crowd cheering. The royal family had arrived at the stadium.

Next she heard a sound like someone slamming doors. That must be the fireworks beginning.

Then there was a sound like popcorn. That must be the champagne. It was time for the feast.

Then there was a sound like someone turning a key. That must be—Lucy looked up in surprise.

It *was* someone turning a key in a door.

The school principal stood in the doorway. She was panting slightly. "I ran all the way from the stadium," she said. "Your classmates told me you'd been left behind. Mr. Turnpike must not have noticed you! In the future, speak up for yourself! Come on! Let's go!"

The principal spun on her heel and began to jog back toward the stadium.

She stopped when she realized Lucy was not behind her. "Lucy?" she said.

But Lucy shook her head.

"I have to go home to my father," she explained.

The principal shrugged. "Suit yourself!" And hurried away.

The long walk home was quieter than a cave. The streets were bare. The whole town was at the stadium.

Actually, she could have gone there herself. Lucy's father did not expect her home yet. He *wanted* her to see the royal tour. But she had already missed most of the fun. All that was left was the contest of the Royal Clue.

Lucy passed the skateboard park. There were the silver letters, spray-painted on the concrete. SECRETS, they whispered to Lucy.

Lucy passed the video arcade. There were the silver lights strung along the awnings. SECRETS, they flickered to Lucy.

At this very moment, Lucy thought, *the most talented people in the town are lining up at the stadium. Each will take a turn at the microphone. Each will give an answer to the Royal Clue. Whoever gets it right will win the prize.*

The prize was an estate in the southern climes. On the estate, there was a small castle, a maple-tree orchard, an ice-skating rink, and a vineyard.

Lucy passed the candy shop. SECRETS, smiled the window.

Lucy did not like her town's most talented people. She did not want to see them win the prize. The winner would be smug and proud, while the other talented people would be cranky.

Lucy passed the nursery school. The silver letters shone at her from the sandbox. SECRETS, they seemed to shrug.

Now if a child *could win the prize*, Lucy thought, *that would be different*. She was sure that a child would not be smug. A child would invite all the other children to *visit* the estate. A child would send a carriage to collect the other children. Lucy could bring her father along! He could take the maple candy of the southern climes! His coughing sickness would be cured!

But, of course, no child would win the prize.

Lucy passed the ice-cream parlor. The silver letters stood on the roof. SECRETS, they said, sighing and looking somber.

She wondered if Mr. Turnpike really knew the answer to the Royal Clue. If not, he would return to school in a temper.

Lucy stopped when she reached the playground. The silver letters were still hanging from the top bar of the jungle gym. SECRETS, they muttered gloomily.

She stared at the letters.

If Mr. Turnpike does not win, she thought, *he'll spend every moment of every day playing the in-between game*. Lucy would never escape it.

Unless, of course, she really *was* the in-between girl. Then she could find a way to fit between her classmates' linked arms. That would surprise Mr. Turnpike!

She looked down at the grass at her feet. If she just concentrated, perhaps she could fit between these blades of grass. There must be a way! *What's the secret?* she wondered, and looked back at the letters.

What secrets do you mean? she asked the letters.

The letters swayed in the breeze. The E clinked gently against the C, and then was silent again.

Perhaps if I could find a way between the letters, Lucy thought helplessly. She stared at the empty space between the S and E, and then at the space between —

She stopped.

Had she imagined that?

A word had leaped into her head.

The word was *Looking*.

Lucy's eyes returned to the space between the S and the E. Was there really a word? She moved closer to the jungle gym and tilted her head this way and that. And then she found it again.

Looking. The word was printed on a tiny piece of cardboard. The cardboard was attached to a tree several feet back from the jungle gym. If you looked between the S and the E with your head at just the right tilt, you could see it clearly.

Feeling odd, Lucy shifted her gaze to the space between the E and the C. Another word leaped out at her. This time the word was *for*. It was printed, she realized, on a fence post at the edge of the park.

Next she tried the space between the C and the R. It took a little longer, but there was another word: *the*. This one was also on cardboard, glued to a red mailbox.

So, she thought, pausing for a moment. That was three words. *Looking for the*.

Between the R and the E, she found the word *in-*.

Between the E and the T, she found the word *between*.

Between the T and the S, she found the word *girl*.

Looking for the in-between girl.

It was impossible. It *must* be her imagination!

But already she was running back the way she had just come. She raced past the ice-cream parlor, the nursery school, the candy shop, the video arcade, and the skateboard park. She reached her own school and slowed.

What if it *was* her imagination? She'd been thinking such strange thoughts about fitting in between. And she had not eaten all day. Perhaps she had gone mad?

There, in her school grounds, was the wooden bench that Mr. Turnpike had first seen. The silver letters were pressed into the seat: SECRETS, they said hopefully.

Lucy ran toward the bench. She hesitated. The letters themselves were scratched and battered from Mr. Turnpike's attacks on them.

She stared carefully at the space between the letters.

Nothing.

Nothing but the green flaking paint of the bench.

She sat on the bench.

Miserable, she scratched at the paint between the s and the E. It flaked away in layers. She kept scratching. Her fingernail found something smooth.

It was a tiny piece of cardboard embedded in the wood. *Looking*, said the cardboard.

It took only a few moments for Lucy to find cardboard between each of the letters. Each piece of cardboard contained a word. Together they made a sentence: *Looking for the in-between girl.*

Now Lucy was flying.

Her heart was beating wildly, her feet were pounding.

She could hardly breathe by the time she reached the stadium.

What if it were already over? What if the contest was done?

But she saw at once that it was not. The royal family was seated on velvet thrones onstage. A mathematician was standing at the microphone. The town sat in rows in the audience. They were clapping politely as Lucy slipped in.

"No," said the king, leaning forward in his throne. "The Royal Clue does *not* mean 528. But thank you for trying."

"Ohhhhh," the audience said sympathetically.

The mathematician sat down, looking shocked. Just the day before, Lucy had heard him tell everyone he had solved the Royal Clue. He had given a number to each of the letters in the word SECRETS, depending on its place in the alphabet. Then he had mixed the numbers, applied his genius, and presto! It was solved!

But it was not.

A chemist stepped up to the microphone. He was carrying a test tube of fizzy pink liquid.

As the chemist spoke, Lucy found her way to the talented people who were standing just offstage. There were only three left: two skinny men in matching leotards and Mr. Turnpike. He looked extremely cheerful.

"No," said the queen, shifting slightly in her throne. "The Royal Clue does not mean pink lemonade. But I thank you, with all my heart, for your efforts."

Lucy thought she saw the princess covering a yawn.

"Mr. Turnpike," she whispered. "I know the answer to the Clue."

Mr. Turnpike looked down at her. "Shush!" he said, frowning.

The two skinny men had run up to the stage. They had solved the Clue together, they said, and would act out the answer as a pair.

"But, Mr. Turnpike," said Lucy. "Don't you want to win? You'll be able to live in the southern climes! You'll never have to teach again! I can tell you the answer!"

Mr. Turnpike twitched with irritation and continued to watch the stage. The skinny men were miming a charade. They whispered secrets in each other's ears. The audience murmured, confused. The queen bit her lip. Mr. Turnpike giggled to himself.

"No," said the prince. "Thank you for trying, but that—er, performance, is not the answer to the Clue."

"But don't you want to know what we were whispering?" cried one of the men. "We were whispering words like *see* and *test*. Words you make by taking the letters of *secrets*! What do you think?!"

But the prince shook his head, and the audience said, "Ohhhhh."

Mr. Turnpike ran up the stairs onto the stage. He flung his purple cloak behind him and smiled a dazzling smile.

His face glowed with delight.

"*I* have solved the Royal Clue!" he declared. "It was quite simple!"

Lucy saw the king's nostrils flare. The princess rolled her eyes.

"You see," Mr. Turnpike said modestly, "I noticed that all the clues appeared in places where *children* play."

At this, the royal family grew perfectly still. They turned toward Mr. Turnpike.

"And *secrets*," continued Mr. Turnpike, "are whispered! Or not spoken at all!"

He played an imaginary drumroll on the microphone and chuckled to himself.

"And so, the answer is this! Children should be seen and not heard!" He bowed flamboyantly and turned to the royal family.

The family slumped in their thrones again. The queen fanned herself with a program. The prince and princess quietly played rock-paper-scissors. The prince, Lucy thought, was very handsome for a boy of her own age.

"No," said the king. "That's not the answer. Thanks, though."

Mr. Turnpike's face turned as purple as his cloak. He stammered and stamped.

The king waved at a royal guard, and Mr. Turnpike was ushered to the side.

"Is there nobody else?" the queen said politely. "Nobody else has an answer to the Clue?"

Lucy was quiet.

"Because," continued the queen, "if there's nobody else, we'll have to declare that the Clue has not been solved. But thank you for your efforts."

Lucy almost stayed silent.

She almost stayed at the side of the stage and let the contest end.

But she did not.

She ran right up the stairs and reached the microphone. It was much too tall for her. The audience laughed. To Lucy, they seemed like a colorful blur. Her hands began to shake.

"Oh, my!" Mr. Turnpike stepped up to the microphone again. "Your Royal Highnesses, I do apologize! This is one of my students! Tremendously poor! I thought it best you not see her, so I tried to lock her in the classroom today, but I see she has escaped."

Lucy realized that her own class was sitting in the front row. Some of her classmates waved at her.

"Now, then!" Mr. Turnpike scolded Lucy. "Stop wasting the royal family's time!"

But the royal guard pressed Mr. Turnpike aside again. Then the guard politely adjusted the microphone, so that it was low enough for Lucy.

"Little one," the Queen said kindly, "do you know the answer to the Clue?"

"I think so," whispered Lucy. "I think it's—"

She hesitated. She was extremely embarrassed.

"Looking for the in-between girl."

There was silence.

Of course, she was mistaken. She began to step aside.

But now, she sensed that the royal family was on its feet. The family was beaming. The king jumped on the spot, and his crown toppled sideways.

"YES!" exclaimed the family in unison. "*That* is the answer to the Royal Clue!"

At once, Mr. Turnpike was back. He pushed Lucy aside. He bent himself in half so he could speak into the microphone.

"Royal family," he purred. "Again, I apologize. I tried to help this little girl today by telling her the answer to the Clue. It would be *dishonest* of me not to stand up now and declare the answer is mine!" He beamed at Lucy. "Thank you for sharing the answer! Good job. Now run along home to your daddy, all right?"

There was clamor and confusion in the audience.

The princess stepped forward. She raised her hands for silence. She looked up at Mr. Turnpike. She spoke into the microphone, which was just the right height for her.

"So, you solved the Clue, Mr. Turnpike?" she said politely.

"Yes, yes," Mr. Turnpike nodded.

"Would you repeat the answer?" said the princess.

"Looking for the in-between girl." Mr. Turnpike bent down to the microphone. He spoke very smoothly.

"Oh!" said the princess. "Well done. So, just to be quite clear, we are looking for the in-between girl?"

"Quite," Mr. Turnpike agreed impatiently. He was scarcely looking at the princess. He was smiling around at the audience in bliss. He was thinking of his castle in the southern climes.

"Well," continued the princess, and she beckoned Lucy closer. "Isn't *this* the in-between girl?"

Mr. Turnpike sniffed, annoyed, and glanced down at Lucy.

"*Certainly* not!" he cried. "What nonsense! That's just Lucy Gold!"

"But don't you always *call* her the in-between girl?" said the princess, tilting her head to the side.

"NEVER!" shouted Mr. Turnpike. "I have NEVER called this child the in-between girl!"

At this, all Lucy's classmates were on their feet. They had had enough. They chanted as one: "He *does* call her that! He *always* calls Lucy the in-between girl! He's *lying*!"

The princess smiled.

"Yes," she said. "I thought so. I also think that Mr. Turnpike is lying when he says he solved the Clue. Lucy solved the Clue. She is our in-between girl. She is our win—"

But before the princess could finish, Mr. Turnpike had grabbed the microphone from her hand. He lifted the whole stand into the air and swung it from side to side. With one swing, he knocked over Lucy; with the other, the princess went flying.

The audience gasped.

"Why is anybody *listening* to this?" shouted Mr. Turnpike. "The princess is a *child*! King! Queen! Have you noticed how *short* she is? Send her to her room!"

He beat his fists on his head.

The royal guard helped Lucy and the princess to their feet. Then he took Mr. Turnpike's fists and handcuffed them behind his back.

"Your Majesty," Mr. Turnpike pleaded, gazing, teary-eyed, at the queen. "I realize I just made an error in judgment, knocking over the princess. But I'm not very fond of children, you see, and, another thing, I'm allergic to poor people! So, you see, none of this is my fault!"

The queen smiled at him. "Oh, I don't blame you at all," she said calmly. "In fact, I'm going to cure your allergy! I'm sending you to live in a cardboard box. From now on, you will spend your days bringing gifts to poor children. In a decade, you'll be a new man!" She nodded briskly at the royal guard, who marched Mr. Turnpike from the stage. He sobbed, "Your Majesty! No!"

But the queen ignored him. She was glancing back at the talented people, clustered at the side of the stage.

"Didn't it occur to any of you," she said, "that we had put the Clue in all the places where children usually play? So maybe we were looking for a child?"

The talented people looked even crankier. Some hung their heads, ashamed.

The king took the microphone and chatted into it. "The thing is," he said, "our little princess has an allergy of her own. She's allergic to worried children. For weeks now, she's hardly slept a wink, and you know why? Because the children in Mr. Turnpike's class have been tossing and turning in their beds, worrying about the in-between girl. So we decided we'd better come and rescue her!"

"Ladies and gentlemen!" the queen said smoothly. "We thank you all for a wonderful day. You tried very hard. And now we will take our winner to the royal carriage, collect her father, and dine together at their castle in the southern climes. A round of applause, if you please, for the in-between girl!!"

The town leaped into the air. There was clapping, laughing, hoo-hahing, whistling, chanting, and cheering, all for the in-between girl.

Lucy scarcely heard the applause.

The princess was leaning toward her. "Sorry it took so long," she murmured. "And by the way, you don't have to be the in-between girl anymore."

The prince reached out to shake Lucy's hand. "Pleased to meet you, Lucy Gold," he said with a formal bow.

Lucy Gold smiled and said, "Pleased to meet you, too."

Passages

by Angela Shelf Medearis

"Renee Harris! Don't you hear me calling you?"

Renee turned down the volume on her CD player and sighed deeply. Her mother stood at the top of the basement stairs, holding a box stuffed with a mound of crumpled newspaper. The brown box was marked RENEE'S ROOM! FRAGILE! HANDLE WITH CARE!

Her mother looked angry.

"Sorry, Mom! I was listening to my music," Renee said. "I didn't hear you."

"I can't unpack all these boxes by myself," her mother said, sounding weary. "I need some help. Come and get the boxes that go down to your room, okay?"

"Okay." Renee ran up the steep basement steps.

Her mother handed her the box. Then she went out to the rental van to unload even more boxes.

Renee took her box downstairs. She was in no mood to get into another argument with her mother today. They had already had a long and tense discussion about why her parents had kept their divorce plans a secret from her.

Renee didn't understand why they had waited and waited to tell her that their marriage was over and had been for quite some time. They said that knowing about their divorce would have been too difficult for Renee to handle and might have affected her grades. So, it had remained a secret until two weeks after eighth grade was over.

And everything had seemed so normal last month at Renee's middle-school graduation ceremony! Her parents had sat side by side as Renee gave her commencement speech. She remembered them applauding and smiling proudly when she received awards for her work as president of the student council and certificates for being on the "A" honor roll. They even took Renee to her favorite Chinese restaurant to celebrate.

Everything had seemed so normal—or had it been, really? Now that her parents' secret was out, Renee could see that things had been strange at home. Her father had said that his long absences from home were because he was working at a new job in another town and he had to travel a lot. It was too difficult to drive back and forth every day, he said, so he had taken an apartment in the city, near his office and the airport. He had only been coming home every other weekend.

When her father was home, he spent a lot of time with Renee, but they seldom did anything as a family. Renee had thought that was because her mother was so busy, planning lessons and assignments for her fourth-grade students and grading papers.

Then, they told her. About the divorce. And that they were selling their house in Texas. And that Renee and her mother were moving, in less than a month, into her mother's childhood home in Armstead, Ohio!

"We're moving—to Ohio?" Renee said, her head reeling. "I don't believe this!"

"Yes, we're moving to Armstead," her mother said. "Our family has owned that house and the land that surrounds it since 1840. I loved living in that house, Renee."

"But I don't want to move!" Renee said. "Why can't I live here with you, Daddy?"

"I'm sorry," her father said. "My job keeps me away

from home so much that living with me isn't an option. But we'll spend lots of time together during holidays. I promise."

"We thought it would be best if you and I lived closer to my family," her mother said. "That way we can make a fresh start, but in a familiar place, and you'll have your cousins to hang out with, and your aunts and uncles to give you a big extended family."

"You don't care about me or what I want!" Renee said angrily. "I don't want to move! I like living in Texas! I don't want to leave my friends! We've already got next year all planned out, all the classes we're going to take. It was going to be so much fun! Why didn't you tell me about any of this? Why?"

"Renee, we know this is hard for you," her father said. "But we had to keep it a secret. We didn't want you to worry."

What about now? Renee thought. *Why weren't they worried about how I'd feel now?*

"When my grandmother Rosetta died last year and left me the house, we decided then it would be best for us to move," her mother said. "That house is historic, it's close to the Ohio River, and it has a beautiful view. You'll love living there."

"I love living *here*," Renee said stubbornly.

"I know you do, baby," her mother said. "But I've also received a wonderful opportunity—to be the principal of my old school in Armstead, starting in September. You know I've always wanted to be an elementary-school principal. This is the opportunity of a lifetime. We know this is a big lifestyle change for you, Renee, but this is a huge adjustment for us, too."

"All we're asking is that you give Armstead a chance," her father said. "You never know—living in your great-grandmother's home may be the best thing that's ever happened to you."

Renee put the box down on the cement floor of her new bedroom and sat in her creaky desk chair. Her decision to move into the basement instead of her mother's childhood bedroom on the second floor had started yet another argument. Her mother couldn't understand why Renee didn't want to sleep in the pink-and-white, lacy-curtained bedroom that she had herself decorated as a child. Renee thought the walls were the exact same bright bubble-gum pink of a popular stomach medicine. And Renee couldn't stand the dainty, old-fashioned white furniture and the delicate glass figurines that lined the shelves.

Renee much preferred the cool, stone walls and heavy wooden beams that lined the ceiling in the basement. Besides, the basement was so big! Renee could put an old sleeper sofa her mother had discarded, her big oak computer desk, laptop, printer, copier, stereo system, and television all on one end of the room. On the other end, she put her bed, dresser, nightstand, and a well-padded reading chair. It was like having her own apartment! Even with all that, Renee still had plenty of room for her artwork. She put all of her art supplies, her easel, and an old kitchen table against the only wall that had a row of windows near the ceiling.

She couldn't wait to line the blank white walls with the pictures she'd created over the years, and the photographs she'd taken of interesting buildings—she loved architecture—and of trees in Texas. Renee combined her photographs and artwork in her own collage style that featured bright colors and headlines she'd clipped from newspapers and magazines.

This basement room is the only good thing about moving, Renee thought. She couldn't understand her mother's reluctance to even come downstairs. When they had first arrived, her mother came down a few steps and stood there uneasily, almost shuddering as she looked around the room.

"You act like the basement is haunted or something," Renee said as she squeezed around her mother to come downstairs.

"Well, maybe it is," her mother said. "Your great-grandmother Rosetta used to say that her grandmother Angeline told her stories about hearing strange noises coming from the basement when she was a little girl."

"What kind of noises?" Renee asked. She liked that this room may have had something mysterious about it.

"Whispering, and footsteps, and a strange creaking sound like something heavy was being moved. When your great-great grandmother Angeline finally got up enough courage to come downstairs to investigate, she found nothing. Still, her father told her never to go downstairs and to keep what she'd heard a secret."

"That's silly. She hadn't seen anything. Why keep it a secret?" Renee said. "I like it down here, and this is where I want to stay. Anyway, I think it's cool that everyone in the family thinks it's haunted."

Renee brought more boxes downstairs. One was marked RENEE'S PICTURES! EXTRA FRAGILE! She tore open the packing tape and unwrapped the photograph on top. Her father had taken it during a trip to Ohio two years before, when the family came to visit Grandmother Rosetta. Renee had been about eleven years old. She had on a bright orange T-shirt with a goofy yellow cartoon character on the front. Renee smiled. She used to love that T-shirt. She wore it until it was so faded and torn that her mother made her throw it away.

I wonder if anything really lasts? Renee thought.

Renee put the photograph on her bedroom dresser. She tilted her head to one side as she looked at herself in the mirror and compared her face to her mother's and great-grandmother's faces. Renee looked like a younger version of the two women. They all had the same thick, coal-black curly hair, dark brown skin, and sparkling brown eyes. They even shared the same dimpled smile, although Renee's mother hadn't been smiling much, lately.

At first, Renee had thought her mother was just sad because Grandmother Rosetta had died. Her mother's own parents had died when she was a baby, and Grandmother Rosetta had raised her. Now that her parents' secret was out, Renee knew her mother was also sad because her marriage was coming to an end.

Renee unwrapped the rest of the pictures in the box. She put the photographs of her best friends, Sarah Timerman and Rachel James, on the dresser, too. Looking at her friends made her sad and mad all over again. They had spent *hours* making sure they would all have classes together at Emerson

High School next year. Now Renee would have to make new friends at the small high school in Armstead. It just wasn't fair.

Renee moved the last of her boxes downstairs. She found a few picture hangers and a hammer on her worktable, and began hanging up her artwork. She decided to hang the collage she had done of their old house in Texas above her reading chair, near the corner of the basement. She leaned the painting against the overstuffed chair. She took off her shoes and stood on the chair, so she could get close to the wall.

Renee tilted her head to one side, squinted, and used her pencil to mark the perfect spot for the painting. She hammered the nail into the center of the wall. She leaned against the wall and tried to pick up the painting—

—and suddenly the wall moved!

The chair tipped over and Renee lost her balance, slamming into the wall and falling on the floor. A loud creak echoed in the room. Pieces of plaster fell off the wall and rained down around Renee's head and shoulders.

"Ouch!" Renee pushed the chair out of the way. She rubbed her thigh.

"Renee!" her mother shouted from upstairs. "What is going on down there?"

Renee wobbled to her feet and brushed dust and

pieces of plaster out of her hair and off her clothes. Her mother had run downstairs. Renee thought her mother might be angry about the damage to the wall.

But her mother didn't look angry. She was staring behind Renee as if she'd just seen a ghost.

Renee felt a cool wind blowing through her hair. She slowly turned to see what her mother was seeing. The wall was really a door that had been plastered over. Renee looked into a narrow, dark room that was behind the basement wall.

"What in the world is that?" her mother said.

"It looks like a secret room," Renee said. "Mom, hand me that flashlight on my desk."

Her mother handed her the flashlight. Renee squeezed through the narrow opening in the wall. Her mother followed close behind. The beam of the flashlight bounced around the walls of the tiny room.

"What's that on the floor?" her mother said.

"It looks like an old newspaper or something," Renee said. She picked up the tattered piece of paper and followed her mother back out of the room.

"It's a flyer—advertising a two-hundred dollar reward for returning a slave family," her mother said, and read aloud: *Wanted! Washington Reed, his wife, Mary, and his children, Fielding, Matilda, and Malcolm."* Her mother stared down at the crumbling piece of paper.

"What?" Renee said. "What's wrong?"

"This family must have been hidden in this room," her mother said. "That's why everyone thought the basement was haunted."

"You mean—this house was part of the Underground Railroad?" Renee asked, and her mother nodded. "That's so cool! We were just studying the Underground Railroad in history! I had to read a whole book about it—how abolitionists of all races and religions helped runaway slaves by hiding them and helping them get to the North or to Canada so they could be free."

"Well, that certainly explains the ghost stories," her mother said. "The voices and footsteps were the Reed family—and who knows how many others—who were hiding in this room. Our family kept this place a secret to protect the runaway slaves they were helping."

Renee thought of something. Something that had been bothering her for some time. "Mom, that's a *good* secret. Our family risked their lives to help our people find their freedom. That's something to be very proud of. But there are other kinds of secrets.

Secrets that shouldn't be kept. Like how you and dad kept it a secret from me that you were getting divorced and that we were moving here."

"I know it's been hard for you," her mother said.

"Yes, it's very hard," Renee said. "I don't know if it would have been easier if I had known everything you and dad were planning. I just know that, from now on, I'd rather know the truth."

"You're right," her mother said. "I'll try to be completely honest, from now on."

"So, it's a deal, then? No more secrets in the family?"

"It's a deal," her mother said. "No more secrets."

"Thanks, Mom."

"And, Renee—I have to tell you, I'm so proud of the way you're handling everything."

It felt good to hear that.

"So," her mother said, "what do you want to do about this little room?"

Renee knew exactly what she wanted to do. "Let's call the newspaper and tell them about Great-great-grandmother Angeline and about how our family were conductors on the Underground Railroad. It's time the entire world knows about *this* secret!"

Several weeks later, Renee and her mother sat side by side on the floor of the tiny secret room in the basement, reading the local newspaper. The headline read, FAMILY DISCOVERS SECRET ROOM IN HISTORIC HOUSE. A large picture of Renee and her mother standing in the doorway of the room was on the front page.

Renee had created a huge collage that featured a copy of the reward flyer, pictures of Great-grandma Rosetta, and of the family home. *This is something that will last*, Renee thought. *My art, my family history, my family's love – and the truth.* "I think I'll add this article to my collage," Renee said.

"That's a great idea," her mother said. And smiled her dimpled smile.

Bella's Birthday Present

by Nancy Farmer

Bella Weinstein was invisible. People didn't actually bump into her on the street. They saw her well enough to avoid her, but five seconds later they couldn't remember her. Bella made no more impression than a cardboard box.

She met hundreds of children at school, but no one ever invited her home or wanted to visit in return. Teachers didn't call on her. She never got picked for a team. Sometimes even Mom or Dad looked as though they couldn't quite place who she was.

This made Bella extremely shy, for she secretly believed that if you weren't noticed, you probably weren't worth noticing.

Both of Bella's parents were psychiatrists. Dr. Weinstein (Dad) worked with adults. If his patients were too sad or too happy, he gave them pills to make them *just right*. It reminded Bella of the Three Bears. Sometimes the porridge was too hot and sometimes it was too cold. Dad made sure it was *just right* so everyone could live quietly ever after.

Dr. Weinstein (Mom) was a child psychiatrist. She could turn a whine into a smile in under fifteen minutes, and she held the all-time record in stopping temper tantrums (two minutes). Mom, when she noticed Bella at all, was worried by her shyness. She said comforting things like, "Don't worry, darling. Acne goes away when you get older." Or, "Being overweight is normal for your age." Or, "Your hair looks really pretty when you comb it forward, over your ears."

And Bella would look into the mirror and think, *I'm fat. My ears stick out. I'm covered in zits*. She hadn't known this before.

Mom and Dad were extremely popular, and the Weinsteins' beautiful house was full of visitors. The guests had a wonderful time. Bella could hear their laughter all the way up to her bedroom on the third floor.

On her thirteenth birthday, Bella had a gluten-free carrot cake because Mom was into health foods. She blew out all thirteen candles, but she forgot to make a wish. *Oh, well*, thought Bella. *I wouldn't have got it, anyway.* She was used to disappointment. However, one's thirteenth birthday is an important event, especially when it happens on Halloween. A message went out from Bella's heart. It traveled by psychic e-mail until it landed in a most surprising place.

Meanwhile, Bella opened her presents. Mom and Dad gave her games to improve her math skills and Spanish vocabulary. Grandma Weinstein gave her clothes she had liked when she was young. And Aunt Goldie and Uncle Morris put money into her college fund. Mom and Dad's friends didn't give her anything, because they hadn't known it was her birthday.

Quite soon, everyone forgot the reason for the party and settled down for a normal, happy evening at the Weinsteins' house. They had such a good time talking, it wasn't surprising that they didn't hear the front doorbell. Bella answered it instead.

It was dark outside, and a cold wind blew in a drift of autumn leaves. The sky was covered with rushing clouds, and the air was full of the creaking of branches. A tall man in a black cloak waited on the step.

For a long moment, he and Bella stared at each other. "Are you here to see Dr. Weinstein?" said Bella, thinking it was one of Dad's patients. She didn't think he was one of Mom's. He didn't look like anyone's parent. He seemed too old even though his face wasn't wrinkled. His black hair came down over his forehead, like the letter *M*.

"Happy birthday," he whispered in a voice like the wind. He extended a long arm at the end of which was a rectangular box. The black cloak swirled, and the man dissolved into a column of black dust and blew away.

Bella ran back to the living room and grabbed her father's arm. "Dad! Dad! There's a vampire on the porch! He gave me a present!"

Dad looked up and smiled at the box Bella was waving. "FedEx is delivering late," he remarked. He turned back to his friends.

She climbed the stairs to her room. The noise of the party died away and the sounds of the night came in. The wind moaned around the corners of the house and fiddled with the curtains. Bella carefully looked outside. The moon played hide-and-seek with the clouds. Shadows danced under the bushes in the garden. Something heavy left the branches of a tree and flapped off, cawing mournfully.

Inside the birthday box was a letter and a painting.

Dearest Bella, the letter began. *How time does fly! It seems only yesterday I promised to protect you from that curse Great-aunt Lycosa put on you. Your mother really should have invited her to the party.*

Bella looked up. What curse? What party? She thought the painting was ugly. It was a murky mixture of grays and blacks, with a moon veiled by clouds. Beyond a field of snow, in the middle of a forest, was—what? Bella took it over to the lamp, but that, curiously, made the picture even harder to see.

She experimented and found that the farther she went from the lamp, the clearer the picture became. And when she stood by the window in the moonlight, it became clear.

It was a painting of a huge house. One floor sat on another like the layers in a large, untidy cake, and a wide balcony looked over the forest. There was something so lonely and hopeless about the scene that Bella wanted to put it away at once. But when she looked closer, she saw black pennants fluttering on the roof.

They were actually moving.

She heard—very faintly—a door close. Something skipped across the snowfield, and Bella couldn't take her eyes off it. This could not be happening. Pictures do not move, and things in them do not get closer. The creature came up almost to her face, and she screamed and dropped the painting.

"This *is* an improvement," said a scratchy voice.

Bella opened her eyes to see an odd creature. His

arms and legs were like knotted roots, and his head was as round as a coconut. He was sitting on her dresser. As she watched, he casually tipped the lamp over and it crashed to the floor. "I can't tell you how long I've been waiting to do that," he said.

"To smash my lamp?" Bella said faintly. She quickly switched on the ceiling light.

"It's no good breaking things in a picture. Doesn't make the same sound at all."

"You were in the picture?"

"Had to be. That's all that's left of my old mansion. A fine place it was, until the Communists threw your family out."

Bella vaguely remembered something about Mom and Dad coming from Europe, but her parents never talked about their past. "Did the Communists throw you out, too?" she guessed.

"Oh, my. No! They didn't know I was there." The creature chuckled. "I had a wonderful time torment- ing them until they all went mad. They burned the place down and ran off into the forest. That's a place you definitely don't want to be on a snowy night with a pack of hungry wolves."

The creature helped himself to an apple from a bowl of fruit on Bella's desk. He swallowed it from north to south, beginning with the stem. The girl had never seen an apple eaten that way. It made a bulge in the creature's throat as it went down and, after a moment, he made a horrid, retching sound. The apple core shot out of his mouth and landed on the carpet. He put his foot on it.

"I would have been in a pickle if it hadn't been for Tarantula," the creature continued. "She had a painting of the mansion. I moved in until she could find me a proper home."

"Excuse me," Bella said politely. "Would you mind if I cleaned up that apple core?"

"I'd mind it very much." He ground the core in with his heel, making a dark stain on Mom's expensive carpet. Bella bit her lip.

"Who are you?" she asked.

The creature grinned wide enough to fit a banana into his mouth sideways, and sprang onto the bed so suddenly she screamed. "I'm your birthday present. I'm a first-class *kobold* with degrees in irritation, panic, and dread. I can raise goose bumps the size of grapes. There isn't a nightmare I can't ride, and I can outwrestle any monster under a bed, including yours." He bounced up and down so savagely, Bella was afraid the bed would collapse. A moan came from beneath, and a long shadow fled across the rug, dragging many tentacles.

"Get lost, wimp," sneered the creature after the disappearing monster.

"But—but—what is a *kobold*?" gasped Bella, hugging herself and shivering. She'd always known there was a monster there, although Mom and Dad had insisted it was her imagination.

"A *kobold* is a bogeyman. *Your* bogeyman, fortunately, which means you won't have to worry about checking your shoes before putting them on."

"Th-thank you, I guess. Do you have a name?"

"Oh, no, you don't!" said the creature so fiercely the girl retreated to the other side of the bed. "That's how you get rid of *kobolds*. My true name is my business, but you may call me Rumple if you like."

Bella nodded.

"Now get some sleep because you'll need your energy tomorrow." Rumple hopped off the bed, turned sideways, and slid under the door.

Bella swept up the smashed lamp and tried to get the stain out of the carpet. Then she laid out her clothes for school and brushed her teeth—she was an orderly girl—and climbed into bed.

She didn't think she'd be able to sleep after all the excitement, but she felt wonderfully relaxed. For the first time in her life, someone had paid attention to her. Also, it was heaven to lie in a bed without a monster. She slept deeply, only waking once when she heard her mother running down the hall.

"It was in the shower," Mom wailed. "It had

tentacles." Dad's voice rumbled, comforting and reasonable. Bella went back to sleep.

Bogeymen, she discovered in the morning, were only visible to their friends. Mom and Dad didn't see him sitting across from them at breakfast. Rumple stuck his fingers in the honey and drew patterns on the tablecloth. Once, he flicked a piece of toast at Dad's newspaper. Dad lowered the paper and looked puzzled. "Was that you, Bella?"

"No," she said, and gasped because the bogeyman was standing next to Mom. He was pouring the jar of honey into her handbag.

"*Stop*," whispered Bella, but Rumple only stuck his tongue out at her.

"Where's the honey?" said Mom, buttering a piece of toast. "It was here a minute ago."

"Your handbag . . ." Bella began.

"Isn't it nice? It's an Armani, real leopard skin. Did you see that article about attention deficit disorder?" Mom turned to Dad, entirely forgetting Bella's presence.

Armani. Real leopard skin, thought the girl, too stunned to try again.

Bella thought she'd left Rumple behind when she got on the school bus, but he bounced up the steps just before the door closed. "Hot diggity!" he said, licking his lips as he looked at the bus full of children.

"Don't you dare," Bella hissed. "That was a horrible trick you played on Mom."

"It's in my job description: Nasty Surprises R Us." He rolled up and down the aisle like a bowling ball, narrowly missing people's feet. No one saw him.

Bella hated taking the bus. Everyone was part of a group, and she didn't belong. She sat behind a trio of girls who were discussing a birthday party. "I turned thirteen yesterday," Bella said hopefully. The girls looked at her coldly. They shrugged.

"See, that's why I'm here," said Rumple, climbing onto the seat beside her.

"I don't understand," said Bella.

"You're under a curse. When you were born, your parents threw a party," he explained. "They invited six of your seven great-aunts: Tarantula, Nephila, Aranea, Atrax, Marpessa, and Agelena. But they forgot to invite Lycosa. Each of the great-aunts gave you a present—math skills, good ankles, that sort of thing—when Lycosa burst in.

"*'You dare to forget me,'* she cried. *'I curse your child with invisibility!'* Then she stormed out. The other aunts were unable to lift the curse, but they limited it to *social* invisibility. People can see you. They just don't care. Tarantula, who hadn't given her gift yet, vowed to rescue you. Unfortunately, she forgot until your message arrived on the psychic e-mail."

Bella looked up to see the three girls had with-drawn to the other side of the bus. "She's talking to herself," one of them whispered.

"Like a bag lady," another said.

"Time for action," said Rumple. He pulled a bottle from his jacket and sprang to the ceiling. He crawled upside down from one end of the bus to the other, shaking powder over the seats.

Suddenly, a girl jumped up and started scratching wildly. Another and another joined her until every-one—except Bella—was rolling around in the aisle, shrieking and scratching. The driver pulled over and radioed for help.

Rumple dropped down beside Bella. "My special Slidy Itch Powder," he said with a banana-eating grin. He opened his jacket to show a row of pock-ets, each one containing a bottle. "Never-ending Upchuck"—he tapped a lid—"Dandruff Deluxe, BO Enhancer, Instant Zits."

Ambulances arrived and paramedics began treat-ing the students. The three girls pointed at Bella and cried, "She did it! She's the only one who isn't itch-ing!"

"See? You aren't invisible anymore," said Rumple.

"Now they hate me instead. Thanks a lot," said Bella.

A policewoman drove her home. To Bella's surprise, both her parents were waiting and they didn't look happy. "We don't know what happened on the bus," the policewoman said. "Until we do, we want you to keep Bella at home."

When the door closed, both parents turned to their daughter and said, "What on earth has gotten into you?"

"You poured honey into my purse," cried Mom.

"And unplugged the freezer, flooded the attic—" said Dad.

"—filled the washer with mud, and cut up the garden hose," finished Mom.

"You did all that?" Bella yelled at Rumple, who was hanging by his toes from a curtain rail.

"It was a long night. I was bored," said the bogeyman.

"Who are you talking to?" said Mom.

"Him!" Bella pointed at Rumple, who made a rude noise. "Great-aunt Tarantula sent me a bogeyman because I've been cursed, but now everybody hates me and I wish I was dead!" She burst into tears.

Mom and Dad held her between them until she stopped crying. "I told you I saw a monster in the shower last night," said Mom.

"I suppose we'd better tell her," said Dad. He handed Bella a box of tissues, and she blew her nose.

"Tell me what?" Bella sniffled.

"We wanted to make a fresh start when we left the Old Country," said Dad. "We wanted to live where no one knew us and where we wouldn't run into silly prejudices."

"Which old country was that?" said Bella.

"Transylvania. The trouble started when you were born."

"The bogeyman told me about the great-aunts," said Bella.

"Well, it seemed mean not to invite them," said Mom. She poked a broom at the curtain rail, but Rumple had already moved to the fireplace. He kicked ashes onto the rug. "I simply forgot about Lycosa. She's such a *witch*."

"Frankly, she's the reason we left the Old Country," Dad confided. "We always had peasants showing up at the mansion with pitchforks and torches."

"She simply would not leave the locals alone." Mom noticed the ashes on the rug and moved purposefully toward the fireplace. "I mean, how difficult is it to fly to Budapest for dinner?"

"Mom . . ." said Bella, not sure whether she wanted to ask the next question.

"Yes, dearest? Oh, don't worry. The curse has been

lifted. All you needed was a patch of bad behavior to make people notice you. It's called *acting out*. Many teenagers do it."

"Mom, are you and Dad vampires?"

Her parents laughed so heartily, Dad had to sit down and wipe his eyes. "We're *psychiatrists*," he wheezed.

"Drinking blood is so . . . vulgar," said Mom, turning away from the fireplace. Rumple reached out to snag a hole in her stockings, thought better of it, and settled back into the ashes. "It was all right for the great-aunts. They were into cobwebs and mildew. This is America."

"Emotions are every bit as nourishing as blood," Dad explained. "It's a more balanced diet, too."

"The best thing," Mom said, her eyes twinkling, "is that psychiatry is *legal*. Now that the bogeyman has done his job, it's time for him to go back to Transylvania."

"Oh, no, you don't!" said Rumple, leaving a trail of gray blotches as he ran.

"Are you perhaps looking for this?" said Mom, holding up the painting.

Rumple stopped in his tracks. "You can't send me back. I won't go. Bella, you tell them. I was good to you. I cared."

"I thought they had to know your real name," said Bella, who was slightly—but only slightly—sorry for him.

"*She* knows, curse it! She was Great-aunt Tarantula's pet!"

The bogeyman frothed and swore and stamped and threatened, but Mom held the picture up and said very sweetly, "Twinkletoes."

"Now the other bogeymen will laugh at me!" Rumple whizzed around like a balloon losing air and disappeared with a *pop*.

"Don't be upset, dearest, he's in the picture." Mom put her arm around Bella and pointed at the painting where a tiny bogeyman was jumping up and down in the snow. "We'll hang it over the mantel to remind us of how lucky we are."

"Yes, indeed," said Dad. "If Lycosa still lived with us, we'd be run out of town in no time."

That night, the Weinsteins had a candlelight dinner all to themselves. They feasted on chocolate cake and pistachio ice cream, to make up for Bella's disappointing birthday. "You'll never have to eat gluten-free carrot cake again," Mom said. Dad opened a bottle of sparkling cider, and they toasted Bella's new visibility.

The moon shone through the window and onto

the painting over the mantle. Bella heard a tiny sound like a door closing and the faraway crunch of boots on snow.

The shadows at the far end of the room thickened. Dad jumped to his feet, knocking over the cider bottle. Bella saw six tall women—Tarantula, Nephila, Aranea, Atrax, Marpessa, and Agelena, she guessed. Bella smiled to herself. At least life wouldn't be boring from now on.

A seventh shape stepped out of the painting and dropped to the floor as daintily as a spider on a thread.

"Lycosa?" whispered Mom.

"It was cheaper than flying," Lycosa said.

Promise You Won't Tell

by Susan Shreve

Last Thursday, Bea Blue, my new best friend since last Monday, told me a big and important secret. I remember it was Thursday because that's the day the fifth grade has gymnastics, and I hate gymnastics because I'm the only one in the class who can't walk on the balance beam without falling. So, on Thursday after gymnastics, Bea Blue told me that her father was going to prison, and her mother and sister were going to move in with her grandmother maybe forever.

She was crying but quietly crying, so none of the kids in our class took notice of her on her way to the girls' room or the cafeteria or the blacktop.

"Promise you won't tell," she said.

"I cross my heart and hope to die," I said, slipping

my arm over her shoulder, feeling strong and wonderful. I love secrets.

"I'm not telling anyone but you," Bea Blue said.

"I'm so glad," I said, and I meant it completely. Girls don't tell me secrets very often. Not important ones, just secrets that everybody else already knows so it isn't even a secret any longer.

We went out to the blacktop where the other girls were gathering at the edge of the basketball court to talk about boys or about one another or one of the unpopular teachers.

Bea had stopped crying. We sat down on a wrought-iron bench at the other edge of the blacktop, away from the group. We crossed our legs and leaned our elbows on our knees, and Bea told me what had happened.

Her father, who worked in a food store on the night shift, had been stealing money from the cash register for months and even years, and then, a few weeks ago, he was caught.

"Maybe my mom will get a divorce," Bea said. "Maybe my dad will be in prison for a long time. It's very terrible in our house."

I leaned my shoulder into her shoulder, bent my head toward her, and said how awful it must be for her and how glad I was that we were friends.

"Me, too," Bea Blue said. "I don't trust anyone else

to keep a secret except you. Especially the girls in our homeroom."

Bea was one of the popular girls in the class, so I was surprised and pleased to hear she didn't trust the others.

"I can keep a secret forever," I said with a confidence I hadn't earned.

I don't have a very good reputation in my family for secrets. I know that because my brothers tell me that I should learn to keep my mouth shut.

"Tell Daisy something, and you may as well be announcing it on television," my brother Jason says, and that's because I told my mother and my cousin who told my aunt who told my other aunt that Jason's girlfriend had started going out with another boy.

But that, I figured, was my business. Jason is my brother and I have certain rights with family.

When I explained that to Jason, he picked me up by the ankles and held me upside down until I promised I would do anything he asked for a whole year.

So I polished his shoes and took out the trash, which is his job, and walked the dog, which is his job, and cleaned his room and took his laundry to the basement and finally, after two weeks, he forgot about my favors for him.

But I didn't forget my trouble with keeping secrets.

"I can't help it," I said to my mom. "It's like when I can't stop eating chocolate. Every time I hear a secret, I want so much to tell somebody that I can't stop myself."

"You can help it," my mom said. "And if you don't, you won't have any friends."

"Or any brothers."

"You'll have your brothers all your life, but they won't be your friends, either."

In my class at Wooton Elementary in Alexandria, Virginia, there are two groups of girls—these groups don't have names, but I tell my mother that one is called the *In* group and one is called the *Out* group, and I don't belong to either one of them. I fly around the edges of the *In* group hoping to be included, and I stay away from the *Out* group hoping to be ignored. My mother thinks the groups are terrible, but it's been a long time since she was in fifth grade and she may have forgotten there were groups then, and, knowing my mother, she was probably an *In* group girl and that's why she has forgotten. You remember things better when you're the one left out.

Bea Blue is a member of the *In* group.

So I was particularly proud that she had chosen me to hear her secret.

"The thing about so many of my friends is that they talk too much," Bea said to me. "If I told Isabel about my father, she'd have to tell Marie, and even if she told Marie, 'Don't tell,' Marie would write a note to Pansy, and Pansy would tell Ruby. And so everyone would know because Ruby would tell them. That's how she is."

"I know," I said, feeling my face go hot because that's how I am, too, just like Ruby, bursting with Bea Blue's secret in my head.

Ruby was the leader of the *In* group, and she knew everything important.

I liked Ruby well enough, but I didn't like her as much as I would if she liked me—if she even had the time to talk to me in the hall or at gymnastics or after school when we saw each other at the ice-cream shop. The *In* group went to the ice-cream shop together. They went everywhere together.

It occurred to me, sitting across from Ruby in math class after lunch, that if I told her I knew a secret from Bea Blue, I wouldn't have to tell her what the secret was. I could say something like, "Bea Blue is having a bad time."

"How do you know?" Ruby would ask.

"I just know," I'd say.

"Did she tell you?" Ruby would ask.

I'd shrug.

I could drive Ruby crazy this way. And then she'd want to be my friend and hang out with me at the ice-cream shop and I'd go with her, but still I wouldn't have to tell her Bea's important secret.

Bea Blue and I walked home together after school.

"Want to stop by the ice-cream shop?" I asked.

She shook her head.

"All the girls in our class will be there, and I don't feel like sitting around with them."

I was very disappointed but didn't let it show.

"Want to come over to my house?" Bea asked as we crossed Lakehurst Drive to the side of the street where I lived with my mom and dad and three older brothers, so I was the youngest in the family except for the cat, Lucifer. And the only girl.

I didn't know Bea Blue very well, although I admired her from a distance. She wasn't good in sports, but she was a good student and friendly to people, all kinds of people—boys, teachers, even the gym teacher whom no one liked. I knew that she wasn't a "whisperer" like Marie who whispered in someone's ear in front of me, so I could only believe that she was whispering about me. And she wasn't "power happy" like Ruby or cliquey like Jasmine or anything like Sara Jane Hull, who was the prettiest girl in the *In* group but just plain mean.

"I usually don't ask girls in my class over to my house because it's pretty small and maybe they won't like it," Bea said as we turned onto Sage Avenue. There were a lot of shops and apartment buildings. I'd never known anyone who actually lived there.

I was surprised that Bea Blue was worried about the size of her house. She didn't seem the type to care. My house was medium-sized. The main reason I didn't ask the girls in my class over, aside from the fact that the *In* group wouldn't come over, was that my brothers might embarrass me. Especially Jason. He would be likely to say something like, "Daisy's a great kid, but don't bother to tell her anything personal, or it'll be in the newspaper."

We stopped at a redbrick apartment house with a hardware store on the first floor. I'd been to the hardware store many times with my father, but I'd never known that people—such as the Blues—lived above the store, in a two-bedroom apartment that was not only small but depressing and dark.

Bea turned on all the lights, went into the kitchen, checked the cookie jar, which was empty, opened the fridge, which was full of leftovers, and then the freezer, and took out a quart of chocolate-chip ice cream.

"My mom's been too upset to go grocery shopping," she said, spooning out a bowl for both of us.

"I bet."

I sat down cross-legged on the couch, my bowl of ice cream on my knees.

"She's at work and my sister's in high school and no one gets home until after seven o'clock, so I do my homework and eat a snack and sometimes I talk to Ruby or Jasmine on the phone."

Bea Blue was small with curly black hair and wide blue eyes and tiny hands and feet. I noticed those especially.

"I'm glad you came," she said softly.

"Me, too," I said. I didn't exactly know what else to say. She seemed genuinely pleased that I was there and that surprised me. I wasn't accustomed to feeling wanted or needed or important in someone else's life, although of course I had friends and my pain-in-the-neck brothers and my mother and father who loved me. But I was the youngest, the tag-along youngest, the tag-along friend is how I had always felt, as if I were fine enough to have around but basically just an afterthought.

This sudden friendship with Bea Blue was different. I was suspicious of it but also thrilled. More thrilled than worried.

"You know why I told you about my father?"

She had taken off her shoes and socks and was sitting across from me in a rocking chair. Her hair, usually in a ponytail, hung loose around her face.

"I don't know," I said.

"Do you remember last week when I asked you if you were invited to Ruby's birthday party?"

"I remember," I said. Of course, I remembered. I didn't even know that Ruby was having a birthday party, so certainly I hadn't been invited.

"And you said, 'Not yet.'"

"I guess I should have said no."

"I liked that you said 'not yet,' as if you might be invited or, even if you weren't, you wouldn't let me know in case I'd feel sorry for you."

I shrugged, a little embarrassed by Bea's attention.

"You know how suddenly you *like* somebody. That's what happened. Suddenly, I liked you."

"And now we're kind of best friends, right?" I said, burning with self-consciousness and pleasure.

"Right. And I realized that the rest of those girls in the class are okay, but they're not my friends. Not my personal friends. They're just a group of a lot of girls trying to be one girl. You know what I mean?"

"Like everybody has to know everything and be like everybody else and dress the same and talk the same."

"Exactly. And you're different," she said. "You're yourself, and so I knew I could tell you something and you'd never tell anybody."

"You're right," I said. "I wouldn't."

And I was beginning to feel different. I'd never thought of myself as Daisy Ellery, a particular girl with long red hair, braided in a single braid, blue eyes and freckles, long legs and big feet. A girl who is herself.

Sitting on the Blues' nubbly beige couch, I was beginning to grow as if I were actually lengthening from the waist up.

I imagined Ruby calling me on the telephone.

"Hiya, Daisy," she'd say. "We saw you went home with Bea Blue today. What's up with her?"

"Nothing that I know of," I'd reply. "She seemed great to me. Just like always."

And that would be that.

Instinctively I knew, as if some great weight had been lifted off my body, that I was equal to Bea Blue's confidence in me.

I didn't need to tell anyone her secret.

I could keep it forever.

Nancy Werlin

Nancy Werlin is the author of six novels for teenagers, including the Edgar Award–winning mystery *The Killer's Cousin*, *Double Helix*, and her most recent book, *The Rules of Survival*. To find out more about Nancy and her writing, you can visit her Web site at <u>www.nancywerlin.com</u>.

About secrets, Nancy says, "In general, I'm deeply suspicious of people who habitually make and keep secrets. In my story for this anthology, Steffie's secret is a kind of lie—she's concealed who she really is. I believe that if she didn't give up that secret, that lie, her pretense of being someone else would have eventually come true. Her secret would have poisoned her whole self."

Elizabeth Cody Kimmel

Elizabeth Cody Kimmel has written eighteen books for children, which is why she looks tired. Her dream was always to read as many books as possible, and she gets closer to this dream every day. In the seventh grade, she carried around a secret journal called *The Purple Book* and wrote her innermost thoughts in it during class. She still has *The Purple Book* in her office. To her knowledge, no one else has ever read it. Kimmel lives in Cold Spring, New York, with her husband, daughter, and their mystic beagle, Milo. You can visit her Web site at www.cody kimmel.com. Psssssst. . . . Elizabeth Cody Kimmel is desperately afraid of centipedes. Don't tell!

Anne Mazer

Anne Mazer writes: "My story, 'A Lump of Clay,' is based on a moment in seventh-grade art class when I crumpled a clay figurine in my hands and felt as if I had destroyed something alive. I never forgot this moment. When writing the story, I added the figure of Mr. Weevil, who was loosely based on a high school art teacher, and created the totally imaginary ones of Elise and Sara. However, the story had a very different outcome from my own."

Anne Mazer is the author of the Scholastic series The Amazing Days of Abby Hayes and many other books for young readers, including _The Salamander Room_ and _The Oxboy_. She is the editor of four anthologies: _America Street, Going Where I'm Coming From, Working Days_, and _A Walk in My World_. Currently, she is developing a new series for Scholastic.

She lives in Ithaca, New York, with her family.

Lulu Delacre

Lulu Delacre, born in Puerto Rico to Argentinean parents, has written and illustrated many books for children, including the Horn Book Fanfare Book *Arroz con Leche: Popular Songs and Rhymes from Latin America*; *Vejigante Masquerader,* an Américas Award book; and *Golden Tales: Myths, Legends and Folktales from Latin America*, a CCBC Choices Book and an Américas Commended title. *Salsa Stories* made the IRA List of Outstanding International Books. *Rafi and Rosi* and *Rafi and Rosi: Carnival!*, her latest books, are Junior Library Guild selections. Her book, *Arrorró mi niño: Latino Lullabies and Gentle Games*, has won a Pura Belpré Honor for illustration. A common thread in Lulu's work is the celebration of her Latino heritage. Since 1988, she has been living in Silver Spring, Maryland, with her family.

"If You Promise, Never Again" is based on an incident that happened to Lulu when she was Tere's age. However, as in all stories, Lulu turned something true into fiction by mixing the remembered with the imagined.

Janette Rallison

Janette Rallison is the author of five books for young adults, including her latest, *It's a Mall World After All*, and *Fame, Glory, and Other Things on My To-Do List*. She lives in Arizona with her five children, which is where she gets most of her story ideas. (Although she swears no one has turned any stuffed animals to life—yet.)

She has no secrets, partly because her children are all willing to rat on her, and partly because she is lousy at keeping secrets. This is why her husband always figures out beforehand what he'll be getting for Christmas. Should she ever develop any good secrets, you'll find them on her Web site: www.Janette Rallison.com.

Coleen Murtagh Paratore

Coleen Murtagh Paratore is the author of two middle-grade novels, *The Wedding Planner's Daughter* and *The Cupid Chronicles*, and two picture books, *How Prudence Proovit Proved the Truth About Fairy Tales* and *26 BIG Things Small Hands Do*. Five new books are forthcoming. She and her husband and three sons live in Albany, New York, and enjoy long weekends at their beach cottage on Cape Cod, Massachusetts. A popular speaker at schools, libraries, and conferences, it is no "secret" to anyone who knows Coleen how very much she loves to write. www.coleenpara tore.com.

Jaclyn Moriarty

Jaclyn Moriarty is the author of *Feeling Sorry for Celia* and its companion books, *The Year of Secret Assignments* and *The Murder of Bindy Mackenzie*. She grew up in Sydney, Australia, and worked as a media and entertainment lawyer, but now lives in Montreal, Canada (because her husband is Canadian), and writes full-time (because she likes to go to work in her pajamas).

When she was nine years old, Jaclyn wrote a secret on a tiny piece of paper, folded the paper, and hid it inside a yellow seashell. She now forgets what the secret was. If anybody finds this yellow seashell, please send it to Jaclyn at once.

Angela Shelf Medearis

Angela Medearis is the award-winning author of more than eighty books for children, including *Seven Spools of Thread*, *Dancing with the Indians*, *The Freedom Riddle*, and *Skin Deep*. *What Did I Do to Deserve a Sister Like You?* is based on her childhood. Mrs. Medearis is also the author of four cookbooks, and she has written several books about African-American arts and Texas history with her husband, Michael.

She says, "I'm not a big believer in keeping secrets, especially family secrets. I like an open, honest relationship, and that's a hard thing to develop if someone is hiding something. I'm even bad at keeping *good* secrets, such as surprise parties. So, if you don't want me to tell the truth, don't tell me anything at all!"

She lives in Austin, Texas.

Nancy Farmer

Nancy Farmer, whose books have won many awards, including the National Book Award for *The House of the Scorpion*, has this to say:

"I grew up in a hotel on the Mexican border. As an adult, I joined the Peace Corps and went to India, where I taught chemistry and ran a chicken farm. After returning to the United States, I joined a commune of hippies in Berkeley, California. Among other jobs, I hawked newspapers, picked peaches, and worked on an oceanographic vessel, before catching a freighter to Africa in search of romance and adventure. I wound up running a lab on Lake Cabora Bassa in Mozambique, one of the wildest places on the globe. Romance showed up in the shape of Harold Farmer, and we have been happily married for thirty-two years. I suppose I have always led the life of a secret agent. I have always been a plain, rather shy person who blends nicely into the wallpaper. That trait is very useful to an author. People say the most amazing things when they think no one important is listening."

Susan Shreve

Susan Shreve is the author of twenty-nine books for children, the newest of which, *Kiss Me Tomorrow*, is from Arthur A. Levine/Scholastic; twelve adult novels, most recently, *A Student of Living Things*, published by Viking; and five anthologies. She is a professor in the MFA program in creative writing at George Mason University.

She says, "Secrets have always excited me, and I have a terrible time keeping them. I wanted to write about a girl who has this same problem. Secrets burn a hole in her pocket, and she has a bad reputation in her family for 'telling.' But, in this story, she learns the value of a secret—to herself and to the person who entrusted her with it."